MW01148084

Table of Contents

Prologue

Let me begin by saying that I'm just the author of this book. I just happened to hear and put down on paper the most incredible stories of the most incredible people I know. They belong to a different breed of men, they are alphas, they are fearless, and they are borderline crazy. They are goodfellas from Bensonhurst.

Believe it or not, when you meet them in person, they are the nicest people around; they laugh a lot, they have that cool old-school Italian swagger and attire that fascinates people so much. But don't mistake their kindness for weakness—they will beat you senseless in seconds, throw your body into a dumpster and go back to drinking with their buddies like nothing happened.

Some of them go away for several years; some just never get caught. A lot of controversy surrounds them: rumors, tall tales—some of them are true, some are created by the vivid imagination of the crowd. But once a goodfella enters the room, everybody feels his presence. And even when you get too intimidated, you can't show your fear; they have the senses of wild animals and will tear you apart right away. Feel free to show your respect though, they like it, and if you happen to gain their trust and establish a friendly relationship with one of them through offering some free service or helping them out with something, you won't regret it in the future. Just like in *The Godfather,* one hand always washes the other and believe me, when you get in trouble you want that hand to be there for you.

Yes, you can call them the bad guys, you can say that they make all their money by breaking the law (and the FBI will most certainly agree with you, otherwise they wouldn't be spending their afternoons filming all the guests arriving at some funeral parlor or a wedding reception), but let me tell you the truth: they are people just like everybody else, and every single one of them has a reason for choosing the path that they did. It is what they do, not who they are. And this was the main reason why I wanted to write down their stories, not just a regular dry biography based on the facts that everyone can get from the Internet or the FBI files, but real, true stories told by the people who were there. All the names, of course, were changed to protect the innocent; I don't want anybody to go to jail because of the confessions they made. Enjoy!

Chapter 1

“They are not made that way, they are born that way.”

“The best way to enter our business is to be born into it.”

Renzo broke his first bone when he was only two years old. It happened while, standing on top of the toilet seat, he was watching his father shave. You may ask yourself, what kind of a child can break his first bone when he’s only two? A future wiseguy, who now proudly counts twenty-eight broken bones in his body, can. And unlike the first one, the rest of them weren’t unlucky incidents.

“I used to drive my mom crazy!” Renzo is always saying when it comes to his childhood stories. “That poor woman had to go through hell when I was a baby! Do you know that all my family members knew that as soon as I would finish eating from my bottle—and they were glass back then—they had to cover themselves up, because right after my bottle would make those sucking noises when the milk was coming to an end, I would throw the bottle right across the room. And you don’t want that to hit you in the head! It happened once to my father though…”

Renzo still throws glasses across the room, but now he aims at the heads of people who forgot to pay their “bills” on time.

When Renzo didn't even know how to walk yet, he already knew how to barricade himself in a room—a skill sometimes very necessary when you don't want the police or the other fellas to get to you. When his mom would leave him alone in the room, he would bounce in his crib until it would move all the way across the room and block the door. And then it would take his poor mom a good ten minutes to get it open again.

"And it wasn't only my mom who I drove nuts," Renzo says. "Do you know that when my aunt Sylvia, who helped raise me till I was six, was dying from Alzheimer's disease in the hospital, she couldn't recognize anybody, neither her sister, nor her own son, who was ten years older than me. But when I came to see her, she smiled and screamed, 'My Renzo!' And then she made a fist at me! The nurses flipped out; they couldn't believe that she remembered me out of the whole family who came to visit her. I told them it's because I drove that poor woman crazy! And you always remember and love the most the one who gave you the most trouble."

At school Renzo didn't get any better. As a matter of fact, he got worse. Let's begin by saying that the whole school thing didn't make him a happy camper, and to escape going there Renzo would throw up every single morning on the way there. His mother, Brigit, was very worried at first, but when she realized what kind of a game her son was playing, she fixed the problem by taking a change of clothes with her each time she brought him to school. Renzo had to accept the fact that school was inevitable and decided to make the best of it.

"My first grade teacher, Ms. Peterson, was plain crazy. She had a big waste bin, and if a student was misbehaving or came to school unprepared, she would put them in that waste bin and make them sit in it under her desk. And you know, you couldn't sue a teacher for something like that back then. Now kids are so spoiled, and their parents are big whiny bitches as well: 'Oh, Mrs. Smith said that my son is not good at math, she hurt his feelings and discouraged him from studying. Let's sue her!' It's not Mrs. Smith's problem, you moron, it's your son who has a peanut for a brain! They have this fancy "attention deficit disorder" now, and these idiots who they have for doctors prescribe those kids some pills to "help them concentrate." Do you know how my father used to make me concentrate? He would give me a beating! I got a D in school, he wouldn't take me to no fancy doctors! Are you fucking kidding me? He would smack me on the back of the head, 'here, now you can concentrate a little better!' Worked like a charm every time! Made me one of the smartest students in my class!

"Anyway, one time some kid in my class took a dump in her closet. I don't know why he did it, whether he was pissed at her for a low grade she had given him or something else, but the fact was that when she saw the "present" he left her, she went ballistic! She screamed for about a minute and said that she'd find out who did it even if she had to pull down the pants of every student and look at their asses. And what do you know? She started doing it! After she checked several students' asses, the kid finally confessed it was him. I seriously thought Ms. Peterson would kill him right then and there. She had some weird fascination with little kids' butts I guess, because this one time she actually put one of the girls across her knee, pulled her panties down in front of the whole class and spanked her! She would have been so sued or put in jail if this happened now!"

High school just took Renzo's minor misdemeanors to a completely different level. To begin with, he sank a boat. You are going to ask yourself, "What?! How could a high school student sink a boat?" Well, I'm going to tell you the story right now, and you will love it.

It was one of those beautiful park outings on rowboats that the school had organized for its students. Peaceful nature around them, rowboats slowly moving along the river, boys and girls enjoying themselves… but then one of Renzo's school friends, Joey, thought that he might enjoy himself even more if he gripped a branch of one of the low trees hanging above the water, so as to stand still for a minute and capture the moment.

But Joey didn't take into consideration the laws of physics, and his weight made the light rowboat incline to one side. Letting go of the branch wasn't an option either, as he didn't want to fall into the water and look stupid in front of the girls sharing a boat with him. But then his good friend Renzo came right to his rescue: he grabbed Joey's legs, but instead of pulling him back to the boat as he had intended, Renzo added more weight to the side of the boat that was already halfway in the water thanks to Joey; the laws of physics won, and the boat flipped over and sank almost in seconds. The result: four students, including Joey, Renzo and two girls had to swim to the shore.

Renzo got suspended from school for three weeks and one more time found himself talking to the principle, "Renzo, do you know that we've had these boat rides for over twenty years, and not one boat ever sank! How could you even do that? I mean, how could you physically sink a boat?"

Renzo just shrugged, happy about his suspension. *More time to hang out with my friends on the corner*, he thought to himself, leaving the principal's office. But those "corner friends" were the ones who contributed to his troublemaking personality even more.

"We had that class where we had social studies for our first period, and my two friends, who knew that I was supposed to go in there after their home room class was over, decided to scare me. They knew that Joey and I were always sitting in the same spot, next to the radiator right under the window; so what they did was during home room they took a blockbuster (imagine the equivalent of the ¾ of a stick of dynamite that's how big it was!), attached a cigarette without a filter to the fuse, hid it under the radiator and left the class without being even noticed.

"Now imagine us sitting there, having no idea what is about to happen, the teacher is explaining something and suddenly: *Boom!!!* I swear to God, it sounded like a fucking grenade explosion! Everybody freaked out of course and rushed to the door. One student got hurt while trying to get out, and me and Joey were just sitting there and laughing while the burnt paper was flying around us. We knew who did it and found it hilarious, unlike the teachers and the six security guards, who rushed in to get us. They actually handcuffed us and took us to the detention room for interrogation. And I didn't want to rat my friends out, so I just said, 'Do you think we are so stupid to make a bomb and then sit next to it?' They didn't want to listen to any explanations, they knew I was the main troublemaker in school. So yeah, I got suspended for three weeks. Again. Big deal… tell me something that I didn't already know was gonna happen!"

And if this wasn't enough for Renzo, he found another way to piss the dean off. He actually got into his office, stole a book of passes and ran the following scheme for the next two weeks: he would put on a white shirt to look like a nerd, come into the class where one of his friends was, give a pass to the teacher and say that the dean wanted to see so and so. The teacher would let the student go of course, and after Renzo gathered all of his friends together, they would go to the bathroom and smoke. It worked perfectly until one of his friends, who was afraid that he might actually get in big trouble, told on Renzo right in front of the whole class. Luckily for Renzo, who could run very fast, he escaped being tackled and got away with it. Just like he keeps getting away from the feds now.

So if you ever wondered what happened to those crazy Italian kids who would always get in trouble in class, they probably followed one of two paths: they either joined the underground world of the five families or went to play on the opposite side of the tracks and became police officers. Either way, they are still playing cowboys and Indians, only on a grown-up level.

Renzo celebrated his Sweet Sixteen by stealing his first car. He thought it would be really cool if he drove to school in some fancy Chevy Impala convertible and impressed all of the girls. Being a street-savvy kid, Renzo knew that back then it would take about a week for a car to go on the so-called "hot sheet" after it got stolen, so he would steal a car, drive it for about five days and drop it somewhere before the time would come up for the police to start checking its license plate. He was doing really well: high school girls were checking out his always new cars and giving him the eye. But Renzo wasn't aware of the fact that his friends were giving his cars "the eye" as well, and pretty soon Renzo started getting very confused by the fact that the cars couldn't be found where he parked them anymore.

"What the hell?" he would think. "It's way too early for the police to start tracking them… Is someone else stealing my stolen cars??"

And so one day Renzo drove to school as usual, parked his car, but instead of going to class, he hid in the bushes not far from the parking lot, which gave him a perfect view of his surroundings. Twenty minutes later a couple of his friends came up to the car, giggling and looking around, got inside and tried to start the car. Renzo jumped out of his hiding spot and chased the boys down the block. He didn't give them a beating, after all they were his friends, but after that Renzo decided to get his own car so as not to deal with the ball-breakers that were always ready to mess with him.

The whole car-stealing thing, however, really got into Renzo's head, and he got so hooked on the adrenalin rush it gave him that he realized he couldn't stay away from other people's cars for too long.

"I remember I was being chased by the police on Belt Parkway and tried to get away on Exit 14, but I didn't realize that I was doing 60 mph or even 70, while the speed limit was no more than 20 mph. So imagine me and three of my friends in the car, making this crazy turn, and the car started leaning on one side more and more… Everybody started screaming 'Wow! Wowww!!!' And guess what? We flipped, and the car started spinning on the roof like crazy.

"All of us of course scattered like fucking mice, two of my friends went under this big rail that was there and took off, and Sammy and I ran to the shore as fast as we could. There was this big rock over there, and thank God it was low tide because then we were able to hide under the rock. We got really lucky, because the cops called the helicopter and it started circling around the area.

"So here we are, sitting under that fucking rock, it's a pitch-black night, and what do you know? The tide started getting higher and higher. The water started rising up our legs, then our knees, then our waists… We looked at each other, and Sammy said, 'What are we gonna do?' I said, 'What do you mean what are we going to do? I ain't getting arrested for a frigging stolen car! We're staying right here until they leave!' Some more time passed, and the water rose to our chests, then shoulders; it was summer, but it was still freezing cold! And just to make things worse, the helicopter wouldn't leave for shit!

"Some more time passed, and the water reached our necks, then chins… we were sitting under that rock with our faces up so we could just breathe! Sammy was freaking out, 'I ain't dying for a stolen car! I'm gonna come out. Better being arrested than dead!' Thank God in about five or ten minutes the cops left and so did the helicopter, and we could finally come out and go home. I came home at four in the morning, soaking wet, and my mom freaked out of course, 'Renzo! What happened to you? Why are you all wet?'

"'Mom, there was some kid that was drowning in the ocean, and Sammy and I saved him.'

"I mean, what else could I say? 'Hi, Mom, I stole a car, was chased by the cops and had to hide away under a rock?' Of course not.

"'You are a hero!' she said. 'This might actually be in the newspaper!'

"*It'll be in the newspaper all right*, I thought, but I didn't say anything and went upstairs to get some sleep before school. Another fucking night to remember!"

Some people would have had enough of the extreme for the rest of their life, especially taking into consideration that last situation, but Renzo has always thought that life without extreme situations is boring and monotonous. Nothing stopped him from trying something new and crazy every day, whether it was positioning a manhole cover in a way that made a cab driver catch it under his car and drive into the car parked nearby; or helping his friends get away from the cops when their stolen car flipped over and they ran out as fast as they could, leaving their books inside. Renzo knew the guys from his high school and of course didn't want them to get caught; so he took the risk of jumping into the flipped car, grabbed all their books and started walking away exactly when the police arrived.

"Hey, you! What the hell happened here?" an officer asked Renzo.

"I almost got hit by that car, officer! It was moving so fast that it crashed into another car over there, flipped over and stayed on that car's roof! I've never seen anything like it!"

"And where are the guys that were driving it?"

"I don't know, sir, they jumped out and took off. I think they went over there, but I'm not sure, I'm still in shock from what happened!"

There followed his innocent doe eyes and nerdy boy look that confused too many police officers too many times. Renzo was indeed a lucky bastard to get out of situations like this.

However, Renzo never seemed to learn from his mistakes. He didn't really think of them as mistakes but more as proof that he was born to get away with any crime he committed. He was growing to be a perfect criminal indeed: a pretty boy with innocent eyes and the mind of a killer. Quite a scary combination.

Another time he proved himself to be a crazy teenager without any fear happened during one significant evening that he still remembers like it happened yesterday.

My good friend, Tommy's cousin, came to stay with Tommy for the summer. He was hanging out with our crew of course, so he became our buddy, one of us. And soon he started going out with some girl, who one day took him to a bar in Flatbush called Brennan's—it was all Irish back then. You know, us, Italians and them, Irish, weren't too fond of each other, to say the least. And to Tommy's cousin's bad luck, that girl had just broken up with her boyfriend, who was a regular at Brennan's, so she thought that it would be a cool idea to bring her new boyfriend to that bar to make her old one jealous. Or just to show him that a girl like her wouldn't stay alone for a long time. Anyway, Tommy's cousin ended up getting jumped by about ten guys. He came home all bleeding, with a broken nose. They gave him a really bad beating.

So the next day, when Tommy told us what happened, we decided to go to Brennan's and kick those bastards' asses. We jumped into two cars, mine and Tommy's, and took off to Flatbush. We parked on the corner. The streets were narrow there and there was really no parking, so we parked next to a fire hydrant and went inside the bar. Now imagine this, we came in, tough guys, about ten or twelve of us and there's a full bar of Irish guys in there. OK, no big deal.

One of them asks us with a nasty face, "What do you guys want?"

We say, "We want to speak to John." (John was behind the whole beating thing. He was the one who used to date that girl).

Then we see this asshole step up. "I'm John, what the fuck do you want?"

"Let's go outside and talk."

"I ain't going outside. I'm fine right here. Talk."

"No, let's go outside."

So we went back and forth like that, and then I noticed that the bartender started passing baseball bats under the bar. I quickly realized that it's only ten of us and a hundred of them and told one of my friends, who was a huge bodybuilder and always the loudest one, "Curly," (he used to shave his head completely bald, and you know how Italian kids love to give names to everyone) "let's wait for them outside. Sooner or later they'll come out, and we'll get them."

But Curly was all worked up already and was ready for a fight. He wasn't too bright obviously, he was already taking steroids by then, and I was always saying that they burned his brain to the size of a raisin. He wouldn't listen to anybody, but luckily he always listened to me. He was like my personal pit-bull, when I would say, "Easy, Curly," he would just stay by my side and growl, but he wouldn't bite. But if I would say, "Curly, attack!"—forget about it! You're dead!

I somehow reasoned with him to go outside and wait for John and his crew on the corner, in our cars. We had to wait till four in the morning until they finally came out. Oh, how glad we were to see them! You don't understand!

We jumped out of our cars and started running toward them. They realized what was going on and ran to their car parked on the other side of the road. They got inside before we could get them and locked themselves in. We didn't care, we started banging on the windows and doors, hitting the car with chains and bats (oh, we came prepared!), and when the windows started to crack, John started driving away, trying to shake us off. I realized that they were going to get away and yelled to Tommy, "Let's box them in, put your car behind them!"

Meanwhile, I ran to my car and turned it this way, so it would block the road, their only means of escape. So here was this narrow street, my car was in front of them, Tommy's car was blocking their exit in the back—they were locked in.

We started jumping on John's car again, smashing it with baseball bats, and they tried to move back and forth with no results. Curly even jumped onto the hood smashing their windshield, till they quickly backed up, and he fell to the ground. And then John, that asshole, put his foot on the gas trying to run Curly over. Luckily,

I was nearby and grabbed Curly like a kitten by the collar of his shirt and pulled him away from the car.

That "little incident" really pissed me off! You are trying to run my friend over? You are so fucking dead! I jumped on their hood and smashed the front window completely, and then they realized that they were probably going to die tonight. You know, when people realize something like that, they do some crazy shit to stay alive, and that's exactly what they did.

Now listen to this, you'll never hear anything like this in your life: John accelerated so hard going up onto the sidewalk that we all quickly jumped off his car. He kept speeding up on the sidewalk, and since the streets were very narrow and he had to make a quick turn, of course he lost control over the car. It crashed into a tree across the street, ricocheted off it, drove sideways through the front porch of a nearby house, and then smashed into the house itself. I've never seen anything like it!

We all hollered, "Ohhhh, shit!!!"

We jumped into our cars and drove off before the police could come and get us—we had already heard the sirens not too far away. We got away once again! I don't know how, but we did.

Chapter 2

"The 60's generation"

"I have absolutely no pleasure in the stimulants in which I sometimes so madly indulge."

(E.A.Poe)

Thinking of factors that contributed to the undisputable madness inside future wiseguys' heads, I can't blame anything more than experimenting with drugs. Let's face it, the 60's generation was the one that started the hippie movement, the one that was worshiping "The Beatles," Janice Joplin and Jimmy Hendrix, the one that was interchanging their breakfast with acid and dinner with coke. I can honestly say, I wish I was born in the fifties, so I could have witnessed first-hand the happy mess created by the mixture of Quaaludes and "Make Love Not War" slogans. It was a generation that dared to think differently, to invent new music, a new style and a new attitude to life, a very different one from what their parents found acceptable. They were the dreamers, fearless and desperate to make a new world, a world where an individual's inner desires were put above all else, as opposed to the sheepish mentality of the masses imposed on their parents by the Cold War.

Renzo was just a child of his time, just like his older sister, Delilah, who was the one that introduced her little brother to "The Beatles" and made him for the first time realize the band's unbelievable potential and influence on the young generation. He was a little confused watching Delilah cry and scream hysterically while watching the pandemonium of "The Beatles" concert in Shea Stadium, the very first time they performed live on American ground for over 55,000 people... the largest live concert of all time, which still holds the record to this very day. It was probably the first British "invasion" that all American teenagers welcomed so open-heartedly; they surrendered and willingly fell into their British idols' captivity.

Renzo remembers singing "I Am The Walrus" at the top of his lungs while riding his first motorcycle with Delilah holding onto him tightly. He thought he was invincible—a beast that wasn't influenced by any laws of nature. He was young, and when you're young, you always think you're immortal. Young people defy death, they denounce it and the flower generation was the one that simply didn't believe in it anymore. And when you don't believe in death, you try to cheat it and play with it just to prove it wrong.

Renzo thought the same as he was doing at least 100 mph on one of the Brooklyn highways. His new bike had to be tested, and Renzo had planned on getting everything he could out of it. Brooklyn police, however, didn't really approve of testing new bikes at that kind of speed on the respectful neighborhood roads and normally arrested the daredevils who performed such actions. And that's exactly what happened to the siblings: very soon Renzo's "I Am The Walrus" was accompanied by police sirens behind their bike. Of course, the idea of pulling over never even occurred to him, and he pressed the accelerator even more, getting away from the chase. In a couple of minutes, Renzo reached the speed of 140 mph, approaching the tunnel leading to the City; his sister was screaming behind his back—she started to think that if they survived, it would be a miracle.

Not wanting to be intercepted by the police on the other side of the tunnel, Renzo made a sharp turn and missed the concrete wall by only a couple of inches. He headed back to Bensonhurst, taking the streets. This was probably one of those situations in his life when his ability to escape the cops was being mastered to perfection because pretty soon he became a getaway driver for certain "good fellas" of Brooklyn. Being a savvy kid, Renzo took the one-way streets going the wrong way, opposite the traffic, which made the police lose him in a matter of minutes. And everything would have been perfect again, except for the fact that they had his license plate numbers.

I knew that I couldn't go back home on that bike. They would be waiting there for me. So I did the only thing that I could: I went to a friend of mine and asked him for help. I said, "They'll get me, Jimmy, you have to help me!" He did, of course.

He said, "Take your bike to my garage, we'll cover it, and I'll close the doors. They'll never find it." I thanked him a thousand times and told him that I owed him a big one. Then I let my sister go to her girlfriend's, and I went to take care of the last thing that had to be done—covering my ass. I went right to the closest precinct and asked an officer to file a report on the stolen bike. The officer looked at me suspiciously, but I looked him right in the eyes and started saying how upset I was about my new bike, I mean, I just got it, and now someone took it, and that sucks! He signed the form and let me go.

As I was approaching my house, I immediately spotted my father sitting outside with a few police officers. He was looking at me and shaking his head, not a good sign to begin with.

"Good evening, officers," I greeted them. "Has something happened?"

"You bet your ass, something happened!" That was the one who was chasing me on the highway, I thought. "Do you know I was the one that chased your ass at 140 mph on Belt Parkway, and what the hell did you do to that girl who was screaming behind your back? Did you kidnap her or something?"

"First of all, you didn't chase me, sir, you chased the guy who stole my bike."

He was looking me straight in the eye.

"You're saying your bike was stolen? Well, that's convenient! And do you have a police report to prove that?"

And that's when I knew I had him.

"Right here, officer. I just came back from the precinct."

I handed him the paper. He examined it thoroughly and returned it to me, saying, "I know it was you I was chasing… and I'm gonna nail your ass… one way or another I'm going to nail your fast-talking ass… don't let me catch you again on my highway, son!"

He knew what I had done but had nothing to prove it, so he left. And now I had to face my pissed father.

"What did you do to your sister?" was his first question.

"Nothing. She's at her friend's house."

"And what did you do to your bike?"

"Nothing. I let Jimmy ride it."

He just shook his head and let me walk inside the house without smacking me, even though I really deserved it.

"You're too smart for your age and for your own good." That was the only thing he said. In a week I went back to the precinct and told them that I found my bike dumped on the sidewalk in the neighborhood. But I didn't go back to that highway for a long time!

It was “Sex, Drugs and Rock-n-Roll” for those kids. All of life was just a big party where the more fucked-up you got, the merrier it seemed. They were experimenting with everything they could find, and their unstable teenage psyches were reacting accordingly. Sometimes it didn’t end too well, just like one time when Renzo and a couple of his friends were hanging out on the roof of one of the buildings around the corner from them. Renzo and Vinnie were drinking wine, unlike Paul, who was into every type of drug he could get. But since he couldn’t afford anything fancy, he was sniffing glue out of a paper bag. Though sniffing glue was not a great idea to begin with, smoking while doing it was the thing that made the night go wrong. Hot ashes from Paul’s cigarette landed right in the paper bag, and if you’re in any way familiar with glue, you probably know how highly flammable it is.

“Oh, shit!” Paul yelled. He was already too gone to think clearly, so out of a childish instinct, he decided to blow inside the bag to put out the fire. And that’s when the hot burning glue sprayed right onto his face.

For a moment Paul didn’t really realize what was going on, that’s how messed up he was. Renzo and Vinnie, drunk in a half-conscious state, were just sitting there watching their friend’s face burn. Finally Paul felt the heat on his skin and started screaming, trying to get the glue off his face. His friends finally came out of their initial shock and helped Paul put the flames out. They got him to the hospital right away, with severe burns on his cheeks and forehead. He got lucky though: thanks to the immediate medical help, he was scarred only for a couple of years till the burns got lighter and lighter and finally almost disappeared. That taught Renzo to never touch glue in his life.

However, nobody ever got their faces burnt because of any of the other drugs, Renzo thought, when for the first time he put a tiny piece of acid on his tongue. *I'll just try it once. What can possibly happen?* he thought to himself that night. That summer, Renzo and his buddies from the corner Smiley and Sammy were enjoying the sunset near the marina in Sammy's Corvair. They were listening to the radio and watching the stars, when it finally hit them. First Sammy caught delusions and started pointing in the direction of one of the cruise boats to his friends.

"I can see their faces!!! I can see every single passenger on the boat! Do you see them, guys?"

"What are you talking about?" Renzo said, not really feeling the effect of the drug yet but just observing his friend flipping out. "The boat is miles away! How can you possibly see any faces? I don't even see people!"

"I'm telling you, I see their faces in the windows! They're waving at me! I see beautiful girls drinking champagne and men dancing with them! They are waving right now!"

Renzo was laughing at Sammy, until Sammy turned to Smiley to ask his opinion about the faces in the windows and got completely carried away.

"Smiley, you're green!" Sammy started yelling. "What the hell happened to you?"

Renzo burst out laughing, but Sammy couldn't leave the situation with his friend, who had suddenly turned green, unresolved, so he started punching Smiley in the face.

"Smiley! Why the fuck are you green?! Talk to me, buddy! Why the hell is your face green?!"

Renzo was laughing so hard that tears started streaming down his face.

"What the fuck are you doing, Sam?" Renzo said. "Stop punching him!"

"But he's green!!!"

Suddenly, Sammy completely flipped out, jumped out of the car and ran away, leaving behind his friends and his car. The bad news for them was that Sammy had the car keys with him, so there was no way they could drive home. They waited for him for several hours, Renzo still laughing and Smiley holding a handkerchief on top of his bleeding nose. At sunrise, after they finally sobered up and still hadn't gotten any news from Sammy, they had no other option than to leave the car behind and walk home.

Sammy came back three days later, all dirty, stinky and sporting a beard. His friends asked all kinds of questions about where he had been and what he had been doing, but he just kept answering with the same thing, "I have no idea!" The only thing he remembered was that he woke up somewhere upstate and had to take a train to go back to Brooklyn. It didn't stop him from doing more acid in the future though.

Drinking and drug abuse was one of the reasons why those young guys were so messed up. No wonder, taking into consideration the fact that they started drinking at thirteen or fourteen. Drinking was the official "baptizing" ritual among the boys from Bensonhurst. Their parents couldn't really devote too much time to watching their kids: most of them were first or second generation Italian immigrants, and they were busy making money for the family. So the kids were mostly by themselves the whole time. And they all grew up together, like one big family; just like a bunch of brothers, inseparable no matter what. And just like brothers, they teased and pranked each other quite often, most of the time not thinking of the consequences. Truthfully, if Renzo had to pay a dollar for every time he would think of the consequences… well, he would have been broke. And that was the smartest kid in the whole crew.

They didn't really care, they were young, crazy and just wanted to have fun. And as the well-known saying goes, no good story ever started with "Once I had a salad and..." Alcohol was the irreplaceable sponsor behind their sick stories, which became almost legendary as they are still proudly told from grandfather to grandson (or son, as most of those nutty kids from the 60s are still too young to be grandparents). Here's one of those stories, told by Renzo himself in order to make sure that all the details are accurate—no normal writer would actually be able to come up with something like this.

This guy's name was Pete, and he could drink! I mean, really drink! Every time we would go out, he could easily finish a good pint of vodka by himself and sometimes even more than that. So this one time my buddy Joey and I decided to prank him.

We were at Joe's house, when I called Pete and said, "Pete, I bet you a hundred dollars that Joey can outdrink you!"

Of course he started laughing, as Joe wasn't such a big drinker and would get drunk pretty fast, so he took the bet right away. And what we did prior to him coming over was we emptied Joe's bottle of scotch, put apple juice instead of liquor in it and closed it tightly, so it looked like a new one. Here's Pete, smiling at us, quite sure that he was gonna be a hundred dollars richer in about an hour or so, while Joey and I were trying to keep a straight face and not crack up.

"Here's your bottle of vodka, Pete, and here's your bottle of scotch, Joe. Whoever finishes first, wins a hundred bucks. Go!"

That idiot wasn't suspecting anything of course and started drinking vodka right from the bottle little by little. And every time he would take a break, we kept encouraging him to go faster, "Come on, Pete, look at Joey, he's drank more than you already!"

And he would drink more and more, while Joey was drinking apple juice, can you imagine? We were trying so hard not to start giggling like little kids, I swear to God, it was one of the funniest things I've ever seen in my life! In about an hour they were both done, but Pete was *really* done! Oh, God, he was gone, he couldn't talk, he couldn't stand, and we were just laughing our asses off, until he started throwing up.

"Not on my mother's carpet!" Joe started screaming, and we both dragged Pete into the bathroom.

Joey's mother was a neat freak, everything was spotless in her house. I'm talking freakishly, immaculately clean; you could have done a frigging heart transplant surgery in her bathroom, that's how clean it was! That's why we decided that leaving him there for some time would at least minimize the surface that we would have to clean afterwards, but imagine the degree of our horror when we heard the sound of all those pretty little porcelain statuettes in there being crushed by a half-conscious Pete behind the closed door as he was obviously trying to get to the toilet. But as we saw after getting inside, he never made it.

Picture this: Pete's lying down on the floor, throwing up all over the room and himself, and we just stood there like two idiots, with no idea what to do next. I've never seen so much vomit in my entire life! It was literally everywhere: in the bathtub, on top of the toilet (he was too fucked-up to even open it!), in the sink, on the throw rug, on the towels, walls and even the ceiling!

Joey was in shock. "How the fuck did he make it go to the ceiling?!"

"I don't know, man... I guess he was trying to get some fresh air from the small window up high there and threw up on the way to it!"

"Jesus Christ, we're never gonna clean all of this mess! My mother will kill me! She'll cut me up and stuff me like a fuckin turkey for Thanksgiving!"

Meanwhile Pete was still lying down on the floor, not even making attempts to do his business in one place.

"Man, we have to get him out of here! He just won't stop!" I said to Joey.

Of course he agreed right away. No shit, he was more scared of his mother than all the New York gangsters put together, and he had a good reason to be. The only problem was that we had no idea how to get Pete out, as he was all covered in vomit and there wasn't a chance that we could grab his arms without making a mess out of ourselves as well.

"Let's bring the towels from the kitchen, wrap them around his wrists and drag him out!" I suggested. A brilliant idea (I thought).

"Great! Let's do that!" Joey simply didn't know any better and would have agreed to whatever I had come up with just to get the half-comatose, stinking Pete out of his house.

What we didn't take into consideration was the fact that dragging Pete through the house would leave a vomit trail all over the floor, and when we looked back, it was too late. We were already at the door and there was nothing better we could do, so we just sighed at the thought of how long we were going to clean up later on and just kept dragging Pete down the stairs. And who do you think, to our fuckin luck of course, was parking their car in the driveway? Joey's girl's mother, who lived directly next door, and whose house was attached to Joey's house. Then we really freaked out and just froze there, like two frigging killers caught at a crime scene with the body in their hands!

"What the hell did you do to that boy?!" were the first words that came out of her mouth as soon as she stepped out of the car. "Is he dead? Did you kill him?"

By then Pete had already stopped throwing up all over the place and was just hanging there, looking pretty much like a dead body with the whitish color of his face. So her confusion was quite understandable.

"No, Mrs. Keller, he's just drunk. We're taking him out to get some fresh air." I had to say something, as Joe seemed to lose his voice in sight of the threatening-looking Mrs. Keller. "We'll just put him over there on the grass to freshen up a little."

"Oh, Jesus Christ and Mary! You'd better make sure that he's not dead, you little bastards! Just look at what you morons have done to the poor boy!"

She finally went inside, shaking her head and cursing us out, and we had nothing else to do than to drag Pete to the lawn and start hosing him down to clean him up as much as we could. And after that we spent a couple more hours mopping the floors and the bathroom, which to my opinion would have been easier to burn down and build back again than to get rid of that terrible smell that just wouldn't go away for shit! Finally we finished cleaning, gluing all the porcelain statuettes together and spraying the whole house with air freshener. Then we had one last thing to do: to get Pete home.

He didn't even wake up when we picked him up from the grass, he didn't even move when we dragged him to his car and put him in the back seat. He was unconscious as unconscious could be! But it was actually for the best, as it made our job way easier: as soon as we parked his car in front of his house, we took him upstairs, put him in his bed, covered him with a blanket and ran away like little kids before his parents got home.

And then another sick idea came to our minds: if Pete was already sleeping and there's no chance he'd wake up within the next twelve hours, why don't we take his car for a joy ride? We raced all over the neighborhood laughing and carrying on and challenging every car we met at the light to a race to the next light. We ran that car into the ground until we heard a loud bang and the car stopped moving forward. Me and Joey looked at each other and said, "Now what do we do?" The car wasn't moving, and we were on the other side of frigging Brooklyn!

Joey offered to try all the other gears to see what would happen… strangely enough all the other gears wouldn't work, except reverse! So there was nothing left for us to do but drive home in reverse for miles and miles. Thank God we found the parking spot in front of Pete's house available. We backed right into it, snuck upstairs into his house and put the keys in his vomit-ridden pants then got the fuck out of there before his parents could catch us.

Finally poor Pete came back to our corner (driving in reverse) after four days, and he still looked like shit! When we asked him what had happened, he said that he had been sleeping all this time, the poor bastard! He also said something had happened to his car, and it would only go in reverse now! Me and Joey looked at each other and said, “It’s no wonder, the way you staggered off that night after we begged you not to go. It’s a miracle it even moves at all… and you too!”

Of course we never told him what we did, and he’s still curious why he’s prohibited from Joey’s mom’s house. All in a night’s fun in Bensonhurst!

Another funny drug abuse case took place in the Poconos, where Renzo, his several cousins and their girlfriends were spending the Fourth of July. It was the first time that Renzo tried mescaline, and he would never forget it.

None of us had ever tried it before, so we thought it would be fun if we tried it once. I mean, what could have been better than finally being away from our parents’ homes—we had girls with us, it was the Fourth of July, we were young and stupid… When else would you try it? When you’re fifty? So we did it, and if you’re not familiar with the drug, I’ll tell you what it does: you start laughing uncontrollably. You just can’t stop! And everything you see is hilarious, let alone if someone tells a joke! Of course I had to fuck with everybody, I kept saying funny shit and coming up with stuff that was just too much for everybody to take. My cousin was literally rolling on the floor laughing, and I remember his girl telling me, "Renzo, stop! He can't breathe! You're gonna make him have a heart attack!"

But anyway, it was the Fourth of July, and we had brought a whole box of fireworks with us. Of course we thought we should celebrate our independence by lighting them up. And since we were all on mescaline and too fucked-up to think clearly, we thought it would be funny if we lit up the whole box at once. So I lit a paper napkin and threw it into the box, which took a few seconds to burn and left me enough time to run back to my friends, where I waited for the explosions to begin. Here, to our surprise, we saw the lights of an approaching car. I actually thought that it was a friend of ours that finally made it to our house, and I started waving at him. But it wasn't our friend: as the car drove up, we saw the sheriff markings on the doors, and what were the odds that he had to park right next to the fucking box of fireworks!

The events that took place next would make a great summer blockbuster movie episode: the sheriff opened the door not seeing the box (we were in the mountains and at night you couldn't see shit there), put his foot right inside the box, pushed the burning napkin on top of the fireworks and the whole thing started shooting! The sheriff jumped back inside his car—the fireworks were shooting in every frigging direction imaginable and inside his car as well—and frantically closed the door behind himself. I've never seen such a fireworks display in my entire life!

It continued going off for about five minutes nonstop, and when it was all finally over, we had to face the sheriff. He came out of the car and started yelling at us, "What the hell are you kids doing?!"

"Nothing, sir, it's the Fourth of July, and we just wanted to light up some fireworks," my cousin replied; he was the most coherent of us. The rest of us were trying really hard not to laugh, but the mescaline was still affecting us and we started laughing like little kids.

"Do you know that fireworks are illegal here? You could have killed somebody!"

He lectured us for like ten minutes, but all I could see was his leg half black from the fireworks and the side of his car, which was all messed up. It was too much for me to handle, and I started laughing.

"What are you laughing at, boy? Do you think it's funny? Have you been drinking?"

"No, sir, just a couple of beers, that's all."

"What am I gonna tell them at the office when they ask me about what happened to my car? It's all black now!"

It was all too much for me to handle, and I started laughing hysterically again. Luckily, after lecturing us for another five minutes, the sheriff finally left. It was one of the best Independence Days I've ever had. Once again I cheated the long arm of the law!

The Bensonhurst police didn't really bother with those kids. They were like that themselves when they were teenagers, so they were more than understanding toward Renzo and his friends. They just made sure they didn't really break the law; whatever else the kids were doing, as long as it wasn't considered a felony, didn't really bother them. They had a remarkable sense of humor, those cops, and when Renzo's friend Joe, who seemed to always get into the most trouble (maybe just because he was the one who would always get caught) turned 17—the official age when the police could actually take him to jail instead of just giving him another paper from juvenile hall—the cops came to his hangout, presented him with a little cupcake with a lit candle on top of it and sang him the "Happy Birthday" song. Joe, watching with a very flat face, took it as not such a good sign and stopped all his misbehavior right away.

However, one of the cops, who had just been transferred to the nearby precinct, was not so fond of Renzo and his friends' stunts and decided to lay down the law like some sheriff from the Wild West—a bad, bad idea, as it turned out later.

His name was Officer Stenklovich, and on the very first day of his patrol on a new beat, he came up to Renzo's crew, already well-known and always hanging out on the corner of 86th street, and pronounced the following speech.

"I've been warned about you boys... you have a very bad reputation in the neighborhood, and everybody in the precinct has day dreams about putting you behind bars, you little jerkoffs. I know what you've been up to, and unlike the other officers I'm not gonna tolerate it during my shifts. Fun is officially over, guys. From now on, this is my neighborhood, these are my streets and you, assholes, are not gonna cause me any trouble. I don't care what you do to the other officers on this beat, but your tricks are not gonna fly with me, you got it?"

"Absolutely, sir." Renzo already knew he had to do something with this prick. "I can promise you right here and now, we'll stay right on this corner during your patrol and not cause any more trouble."

"Good. I'm glad we came to an understanding."

With these words Officer Stenklovich stared at Renzo hard for a couple more seconds, then turned around and left.

"Guys." Renzo smiled widely at his buddies. "I think we need to welcome the nice gentleman into our neighborhood just like he deserves. Now who wants to go shopping with me?"

"What are we going to buy?"

"Eggs. A lot of eggs. I want to make a nice welcoming cake for my new friend, Officer Stenky!"

The guys just started giggling; they knew that their main instigator had a plan, and they were more than ready to roll with it.

The young men didn't break their promise though: they did stay exactly on that same corner where they always gathered, but this time, during Officer Stenklovich's next shift, they were three stories higher, at the very top of the roof, loaded with six dozen eggs and waiting for their victim to show up. A happy smile crossed Renzo's face as soon as he saw Stenky walking from across the street, getting closer and closer… He stopped for a moment, obviously confused by the absence of the troublemakers at their usual spot. At the same exact moment, Renzo gave a signal to his buddies, and the first two-dozen eggs hit the target with surprising precision. Within seconds Officer Stenklovich was covered in eggs from top to bottom, and while he was calling for reinforcements, Renzo yelled from the top of the roof, "Who's the boss now, Stenky? Or should we call you Stinky? Yeah, I think this name will fit you much better!"

Right after that a couple more dozen eggs flew right onto the poor cop's head. He couldn't even look up to see where all this mess was coming from and was just trying to hide under the store canopies, which frankly speaking didn't do such a good job as shelter. Credit should be given to the nearby precinct's police; they showed up on the spot within minutes in their patrol car. But as soon as they opened the doors and made an attempt to come out, Renzo and his crew showered them with eggs with such force that both cops, who saw what Stenklovich looked like, said to themselves, "Fuck that!" and jumped right back into the car and drove away from the "egg-hitting" range.

The young men only stopped their "shooting" when they were completely out of eggs. After that, laughing and whistling at soaking wet Stenky, they quickly got away, jumping from one rooftop to another. From what they heard from their neighbors, somehow connected to the police, Stenky became the laughing stock of the precinct and transferred to Manhattan right after that incident. Of course all the cops knew who was behind the egg set up, but they found the whole thing too funny to punish anybody. And besides, the boys were too smart to leave any traces behind them, so once again they got away with an innocent and typically Bensonhurst style scumbag-cop assault.

Eggs played a big part in a teenager's life back then: boys, both young and old, were using them instead of guns to teach someone a lesson, just to play around or even to break up a gang battle. Almost all the roofs were open back then, but even if they weren't, the young burglars-in-training knew just the way to find access to whatever roof they wanted. They used to open the locked roof doors with home-made keys, knives or even their mothers' hair pins; they even used to climb up the telephone poles lined up behind the stores and climb over onto the roofs. As upcoming neighborhood hoods, even before they started one of their usual egg bombings, they would always make sure that they had a backup plan to get away as soon as the situation got "hot."

But even the most flawless plans sometimes have a crack, and that's exactly what happened this one time, when Renzo and his friends were messing around on one of the roofs not too far from their hangout. It was just one of their regular gang battles: rival gangs throwing eggs at each other from one roof to another, while also enjoying the obvious fun of bombing everything in sight on the street. Just like many times before, they of course ran out of eggs, so Renzo and his childhood buddy Ben made a quick trip to the store to get some more "ammunition." Just as they were coming out of the elevator on the sixth floor, they got stopped by one of the tenants of the building, on whose roof they were messing around.

"Where the hell do you think you're going, you little bastards?" The threatening intonation of his voice had the complete opposite effect on Renzo, who didn't like to be threatened by anyone.

"It's none of your fucking business where we're going!" Renzo said.

“Get the hell out of here and make sure I never see your faces here ever again!”

“Or what?”

“Or you’re gonna get shot, that’s what!”

With these words the guy took out a pretty big gun from behind his back and pointed it at the boys, clearly expecting them to shit their pants and run downstairs faster than light, but he didn’t take into consideration that Renzo by that time had seen more guns pointed at him than that poor guy had in his entire life.

“Oh yeah?!” Renzo gave the egg cartons he was holding in front of him to Ben and took a step forward with his hands spread wide apart. “Come on and shoot me! Go on! What are you waiting for? Shoot me, you old prick!”

“I’m warning you, get out, or I’ll do it!”

“Renzo, let’s go!” Ben said. If Ben could’ve pushed himself some more into the elevator door as he tried to get away from the line of fire, he would have become as flat as the door itself. “Renzo! Let’s get the fuck out of here!! Are you fucking crazy… he’s got a gun!”

“Fuck him, Ben! He ain’t got the balls to pull the trigger, or he would have done it already! Come on, why aren’t you shooting?” Renzo obviously wasn’t intimidated at all by the sight of a .38 caliber gun pointed at him and kept stepping closer and closer to the old guy. “If you don’t shoot me right now, I swear, I’m gonna take that fucking gun and shove it up your sissy ass, you motherfucker!”

And just as soon as he made a move to snatch up the gun from the already pretty shaken guy's hands, the guy reacted as fast as he could and quickly slammed the door right in front of Renzo's face.

"Go away now, I'm calling the cops!" That was all they heard from behind the closed door.

"Go ahead, let's see what they're gonna say about that gun of yours, which you threatened a teenager with!"

After that, shocked Ben, who had never seen anything like that in his life before, and grinning Renzo, who didn't lose his cool throughout the whole showdown, proceeded to the roof with their eggs to finish their egg battle. They never heard from that neighbor again. Some people say he moved away soon after.

Chapter 3

"The Pool Room"

"A little violence never hurt anyone."

(B.Ruggiero)

Winter came, and now Renzo and his friends had to relocate from their corner at 85th street and 21st Ave to some place warm. Luckily for them, right around the corner there was a big pool room with over fifty tables, which was a famous wiseguy hangout at the time. And that's when Renzo's transformation from a regular Bensonhurst bad boy into a future goodfella really started. They were young and hungry for attention, they wanted to make a name for themselves, they wanted recognition and notoriety. And guys like that were always more than welcome in the Pool Room.

The older wiseguys, who were regulars in the Pool Room, controlled the whole place, despite the fact that the owner was a former detective. However, he was a pretty corrupt cop, quite often bribed by the same wiseguys, so they had more than just a mutual understanding. The bribing worked out fine back in those days; several cases were dropped, and several pairs of eyes were closed when someone undesirable was on his way to upstate New York in his executors' trunk. Those cops all had different reasons for taking bribes: some of them were really in need of money for their big families, some were just plain greedy and didn't want to miss the opportunity to put some extra un-taxable cash in their pockets… so it was kind of a win-win situation for everybody.

The Pool Room for those goodfellas was the perfect place to blow off steam: drinking, playing pool, fighting with each other and abusing the youngsters. Abusing was a little bit of the initiation process for those who had balls big enough to play major league with the "professionals," so a lot of younger boys got their head shoved into the toilet and the water flushed on them, some just got away with little bruises from pool balls thrown at them or sticks broken on their backs. Needless to say, Renzo and his friends wanted to become one of those guys (obviously, the guys who shoved people's heads in the toilet, not the ones who had to go back home stinking).

So pretty soon, after they got accepted and became part of the "gang," they enjoyed all the benefits of their newly-acquired "membership," including the famous "Blackout Ball Fight." Now for those of you who are wondering what the hell that is, let me explain it to you in detail: at some point in the night, somebody killed the main control that powered all the light fixtures, and what you had to do was hide behind the tables because that was the official signal to start the ball fight. The heavy, ivory-made pool balls flew all over the room, and all you heard were screams from all over the place. The whole madness continued for about a minute, and after the lights went back on, all the participants got up from underneath their tables, some of them sporting a new black eye, some with bleeding heads or broken noses. The winner was the one who didn't have any marks on him, and that lucky guy got a free drink on the house and, more importantly, the respect of his peers.

Back then there were five gangs hanging out in the Pool Room: 85th St. & 21st Ave, 85th St. & 20th Ave, Big Louisiana, Little Louisiana and the last one was Little Bath Beach. When my "corner" friend Donny first brought me there, I was part of

85th St. & 21st Ave. They were the calmer guys, if you could apply the term "calmer" to those kind of guys. But later on, when I really started drinking and carrying on, I started getting crazier and crazier and wanted to make a name for myself, so I told Donny that I was gonna go with his Big Louisiana gang, which consisted only of the nuttiest guys in the neighborhood that you could possibly find.

First, I started off as a regular shy high school boy, but pretty soon I got transformed into that out of control kid who everyone was afraid of, who you never knew what he was gonna do next. Even my friends from my gang told me, "Renzo, when you're drunk, you get too crazy! Take it easy, you might get in trouble someday."

But I didn't care, I used to say that trouble was my middle name, and "too crazy" was exactly what I was going for. So they had to leave me alone.

The Pool Room was where Renzo's first acquaintance with the Brooklyn mob world started. But to create a real name for himself and the members of his gang, "Big Louisiana," Renzo had to push the boundaries a little further. And that's when the real craziness began.

We had a ritual in the Pool Room, you know, when at the beginning of the evening all the gangs would get together, have a little drink or two and then go to different locations to do some crazy shit, so that later on we could all come back to the Pool Room and tell each other stories of who did what. Some of those stories got into the papers too! We were anything but normal kids, God, just to think about what we did! One of those nights I got shot, but I'll come back to that later.

One day we decided to pull the following maneuver: me and my buddies from our gang (overall, we had about ten people, five in each car) decided to go to a restaurant in Long Island, it was called Howard Johnson's. So we were drinking there and carrying on, eating and ordering almost everything they had on the menu, for about four hours. Then, when it was time to pay the bill, which was tremendous for those times (about $500-$600), I told the guys who were the drivers that night, "Go to the cars, start them and pull up close to the entrance, but not too close that the management would suspect anything."

Then, I told the other guys to start exiting the restaurant, while me and my two other buddies messed around with the bill, pretending we were "kicking in" to pay it. Of course, we weren't going to pay it!

Anyway, when it was time to give it to the waiter, we went all the way to the entrance where the manager was and I gave my guys a sign to start walking out, while the manager was watching us very closely.

"I know what you're doing," he said. "Don't even think about it."

"What are you talking about?" I said, looking at him with little baby deer eyes and still acting like I was clumsy with my money. "I have it right here, I just can't get it out."

And with these final words, I pushed him away and started running to our cars like there was no tomorrow!

The funniest part was that my guys had already started pulling away and driving, and my buddy who was running next to me was so fat that he couldn't catch the car. And by that time we had all the waiters and managers chasing us, trying to grab that poor fella! I jumped into our car as fast as I could and was trying to drag him in there, but he was so heavy that his legs were actually dragging on the street till me and my buddies finally got him inside. God, was that funny! But I wouldn't do that now of course, now they're smart, they've got cameras everywhere. I'm just kidding, thank God. I can afford a $600 dinner now.

That wasn't the first time one of Renzo's friends had a problem with a car. His name was Sal, and he tested more drugs on himself than a small chemical plant produced. One night, Sal was hanging out with Renzo and some other guys in a bar right across the street from the current Ponte Vecchio restaurant, and he got the idea that a party wasn't a party without some coke and Quaaludes. Top it all off with 40% alcohol, and you had yourself a perfect scenario for a disaster.

But Sal wasn't feeling any pain for quite a long time (time enough to kill a healthy horse with the amount of drugs he did that night, but those Italians just won't die for shit!), until it finally hit him, and he decided to go home and lay down. To all his friends' arguments—there was no fuckin way he could drive in that condition—the stumbling, staggering and simply ossified Sal just made a dismissive move with his hand (at that point he couldn't even talk as the Quaaludes had completely paralyzed his speech organs, making him sound like a suffocating, drunken cow underwater) and got into his car. Now his main goal was to look cool in front of his friends and to prove to them he could drive "just fine," even if the amount of drugs and alcohol in his blood stream actually exceeded the blood itself.

However, he couldn't even manage a simple task like making a U-turn to get across the street and occupy the right lane. His legs were so stiff from the combination of coke and Quaaludes, and his brain was just too slow to react. Those unfortunate factors contributed to the following incident: with his leg stuck on the accelerator, Sal drove right across the street, and obviously forgetting to turn the wheel, drove right into a bar full of people. He smashed through the windows, the bar itself and kept driving even while the unsuspecting people were falling off his hood. When Sal finally stopped and got out of the car, so many pills fell out of his driver's door that those same people who just got hit, jumped on them trying to at least make up for a ruined night with a pocket full of pills. They were as crazy as

Renzo and his friends; so much so that getting hit by a car that drove through their bar barely fazed them.

Meanwhile Sal staggered out of the bar like nothing had happened. The next day he came to see the owners (who, unluckily for Sal, by some coincidence were very influential wiseguys) to tell them that his car had been stolen.

"Sal," one of them said. "We actually saw you getting out of the car last night! You're lucky that nobody got killed! But since we know you and respect the people you're associated with, we won't give you away to the cops if you pay us all the expenses for the repair work and lost business that the insurance won't cover. We'll even confirm to your insurance company that your car was stolen, so you can even get some money back. But you'll have to pay us in full."

That's a pretty sweet deal if you had just driven through a wiseguy hangout, and sober Sal took it without any hesitations. Of course it took him quite a long time to pay everything back, but he did. And if you're curious to know if he stopped doing drugs, or at least driving around under the influence, the answer is no. He did it up until the day he died from a drug overdose.

I used to always say that if you want to see a real nut, go workout with Ben! He was crazy, and I mean big-time crazy! We've known each other since we were born and our mothers used to push our baby carriages together—that's how long we've been friends! And of course we did everything together. We started working out in the same gym at fifteen or sixteen, and he was a monster! His arms, back and neck were so huge that even I couldn't come close to him, even though I had pretty big arms and a big back myself. But he was taking steroids, which messed him up a little bit and made him even crazier than he originally was. I mean, who else would shoot a girl, who was cheating on him with some guy, in the pussy? And then shoot the guy too? And he killed the guy—didn't just shoot off his dick, even though personally I think being dead is much better than walking around with no dick.

He had to go to prison of course, but the funniest part was that it was his ex-girlfriend who actually covered for him; she told the jury and the judge that it was self-defense; that Ben had to shoot because the guy had tried to stab him with a kitchen knife. She didn't do it because of her good and all-forgiving heart, not at all. She just knew that if Ben was convicted for homicide and had to go to jail for twenty years, he would kill her as soon as he got out. So the whole self-defense thing worked out pretty well, and he only had to do five years for the manslaughter charge, which wasn't too bad.

So when he finally got out, I picked him up right from the jail and drove him back to the neighborhood to get some drinks. Sammy and I—Sammy was also in the car with me when I went to pick Ben up—even got Ben a hooker, who gave him a blowjob right in the back seat, while Sammy and I drove laughing like little kids in the front. It was uncomfortable and funny at the same time.

So anyway, it was evening, and we were trying to get to some bar. At that time though the dress code was too strict, and you couldn't get in unless you were wearing a suit or at least a nice sports jacket. For the obvious reason that Ben was just out of jail, he was not dressed to kill, and so we got rejected from several bars. I started to get aggravated and decided to go to a bar managed by my father's friend Vito, who later became one of my best friends. But what do you think happened? The huge bouncer at the entrance, with the head and brain of a rhino, didn't want to let us in either.

"It's a classy place, folks," he said. "You can't come in here looking like that."

I was tired of the bullshit, so I said, "Just call Vito here."

As soon as Vito came out, we got into the bar in a split second.

We drank and carried on for several hours there, celebrating my buddy finally coming back to us, almost till closing. And this was where all the fun began: we came out of the bar, got in my car and I started it, when Ben thought he saw his ex-girlfriend with some guy. He was so drunk though that he wasn't able to tell a horse's ass from his own hand. But alcohol has such an effect on your brain that you don't normally listen to what other people tell you because you are pretty damn sure that you know better.

So here was my buddy Benny, jumping out of the car, screaming that he was going to kill that asshole and that bitch, while I was yelling at him, "It's not her, Ben!!! Look at the damn girl, it's not her!"

Meanwhile, the guy that Ben was after quickly realized that if he didn't get away now, he'd probably get killed right where he was, so he started running. Ben jumped onto the hood of my car, slid on it like in some action movie and started chasing him. That guy's girl saved the situation when she started screaming, because Ben took his time to look at her and to tell her to shut the fuck up before he killed her, and then he finally saw that it wasn't his ex. Vito and I quickly got Ben in the back seat, and I drove the hell out of there before someone could call the cops!

I don't know what was wrong with us. Maybe we were drinking too much, maybe it was our hot Italian blood, but we just couldn't stay out of trouble. But there were fun times too, I mean fun without gangs and shooting! For example, there was the most extreme thing, which they don't do anymore, called Midnight Madness in Coney Island, when they made the Cyclone roller coaster go backwards so that you basically were riding a roller coaster without seeing where you're going! One of my friends, Tom, did a handstand at the highest point of the Cyclone, by the way. That's how crazy we all were! We would ride that roller coaster over and over again. We were drugged out or drunk most of the time, so we just went again and again until we got tired.

There was another great place, where we were always more than welcome. It was called Camelot Inn, and all the coolest bands of that time played there: Frankie Valli, J and the Americans, the Drifters, the Dupree's, the Flamingos and many, many more. I was already working with my father's sign shop at that time. I actually started working pretty early, my first job was at a men's hair salon on 86th street where I helped them clean the floor. I got very good tips from the customers for that, so at nine I was already making about $20 a day.

Later on when I turned 16, I became good friends with a German guy, named Ken Meyer, one of my father's workers, who was also a bouncer at the Camelot Inn. He always let me and my friends in, no IDs, no questions asked. And at that time you had to be eighteen to drink, but the owners sold us alcohol without any problems. We had a really good time there and spent good money too. Even though we were so young, they treated us like gold, but not just because we were regular customers with thick wallets. No, they sometimes didn't even charge us for half of the drinks; they respected us because of the wiseguys we were associated with and because of the name that we had already made for ourselves with all our crazy stories, which followed us wherever we went.

We really enjoyed ourselves there; we sang along with the bands, and pretty soon they started giving us the mic so we could sing some parts of their songs by ourselves. All of us were very talented kids, and we had pretty good voices. Those older guys loved it! Sometimes the singers called us over to their table, and we hung out with them till the end of the night. It was a fabulous place indeed!

Fights? Of course there were fights after leaving the club, and during one of those fights between two gangs, Renzo got his first bullet. Those were the real gang wars back then, not like now, and those kids came at each other with huge knives, guns and baseball bats. It was a war for dominance, and they were out there to kill, to show who had the biggest balls, who wasn't afraid to shoot or get shot. And when the shootings would begin, which was normally at night for obvious reasons, both gangs would start shooting right and left, almost as if they were cowboys in the good old Wild West, but instead of cowboy hats they wore fedoras.

In the heat of the gunfight, Renzo didn't even notice that someone had shot him in the leg, and only a couple of minutes later, after someone from the neighborhood called the cops and they started running away, did he feel the blood streaming down his leg. *What the hell?* Renzo thought. *How did this shit happen?* He couldn't go to the hospital of course, they had a protocol to call the police for interrogation in every case concerning a gunshot wound.

But luckily for him, his friend Ricko was the son of the famous doctor among their circle of wiseguys who everybody just called "Doc." Nobody, except for the people personally referred to the Doc, had any idea what was going on down in his basement, where he, a skilled surgeon, patched everybody up without any questions asked. He was a personal wiseguy doctor, and Renzo finally made a personal acquaintance with him. Renzo wished it would have happened on some more cheerful event, like someone's birthday or a wedding, but as they say, you can't escape your own fate.

Renzo got really lucky, as the bullet hadn't hit any important arteries in his upper leg, otherwise he would have bled to death in just minutes. Instead, that same night he walked home, limping but all on his own, and when his mother questioned what happened to his leg, he told her that he had drilled it in his father's shop. He never found out who shot him, it was almost impossible to find out, as everyone had been shooting each other in the pitch-black of night, and all the guns after that were quickly dumped into the ocean. Luckily for their owners no such thing as forensics existed at that time, and simply wiping their fingerprints off and then dumping their guns was more than enough for the police to never connect them to anything that had happened that night. Renzo still has a little round white scar on his leg, just to remind him of the good old times. But even as tough as he is, he's very happy that it is his only round scar.

The Pool Room was the home for all the nuts out there; all the Bensonhurst daredevils considered it their Mecca for a reason—they went there for the fun and the gunshots. And when you had so many adrenaline-pumped psychos in one place, it became a perfect recipe for everyday fights. One of those ongoing feuds between two people, who Renzo knew very well, was about to get ugly.

Ben was always hanging out in the Pool Room with Renzo and the other guys from 85th St., but since he was a little on the short side, he was always picked on by a guy from the Little Louisiana gang named Billy Bright. Billy Bright was the complete opposite of a nice person to begin with, but being accompanied by twelve to fifteen gang members all the time only increased the degree of his "being-a-dick-ness" to everybody. And just like all those bullies in high school, he chose Ben as his victim (for no apparent reason I guess, other than to show off in front of his buddies) and referred to him only as "muscle head," "shorty" and "hey, Ben, where did you leave your neck?" The only reason why Ben had to put up with all the bullying was that Billy was always surrounded by his entourage, making it impossible for Ben to give him the good beating he deserved.

"I'll get him one day," Ben would tell Renzo every time Billy started his usual routine. "You'll see how I get back at him. I pray to God every day for just one chance!"

Luckily for Ben and not so luckily for Billy Bright, God did hear Ben's prayers and decided to grant him his wish, maybe as an early Hanukkah present, maybe just because He didn't like Billy personally (no one who knew Billy would blame Him for it). One day on their way out of the Pool Room, Renzo and Ben met Billy Bright going inside with only a couple of his guys. Surprisingly, Billy wasn't as aggressive as he normally was, and instead of his usual sarcastic comments, he just greeted Renzo and Ben with a nod. Renzo was kind of glad that Bright had finally stopped being a total jerk even though they never had anything personal between them—probably just because Bright was intimidated by Renzo's already pretty impressive reputation. As Renzo was walking to his car in a pretty good mood, Ben suddenly stopped and looked him in the eye.

"I have to go back there and straighten it out with that asshole," Ben said, looking very determined. By then Renzo already knew that if Ben got something in his head, there was no turning back. But still he tried to talk his friend out of it.

"Are you sure? I mean, he's not as big a dick as he used to be, he's been quite good lately…"

"I'm sure, Renzo. And with you or without you, I have to do this. I just have to."

After a minute of just looking at each other, Renzo shrugged and said, "If you gotta go, I'll go with you. I mean if this is really what you want…"

"I just have to, buddy, you know? I just have to."

And so they went inside.

Ben asked Renzo to wait downstairs and help him only if something went wrong; he realized that Renzo didn't really have anything against Billy, and he didn't want to get him involved in his "business" with Bright. Renzo was prepared to patiently wait till Ben finally got his revenge, but the wait was soon over when he saw his good friend Ben and Billy beating the shit out of each other, first at the top of the stairs and then rolling down the same stairs without both of them even noticing it. They were like two pit-bulls; as soon as they got into each other's throats, they wouldn't let go till someone died.

Of course such a scene attracted a lot of spectators from the Pool Room, which was always up for such an entertaining event (in their eyes): nothing like seeing a good fight. However, those fights, no matter how chaotic they seemed to be for an outsider, had their own rules: if the two guys were fighting for their own reasons, you couldn't start jumping on top of them, beating up on your friend's opponent. But to the douche bags from Bright's circle those laws seemed to be not so much worth observing, and pretty soon one of Billy's guy Gangi started getting on top of Ben, trying to kick him in the ribs and punch him in his head to knock him out. Renzo had no respect for such low moves, even in his young years, so after grabbing the guy by his shirt collar, he threw him across the room like a rag doll.

"They are straightening their own thing out!" Renzo shouted. "Don't jap out my friend, it's between the two of them, you piece of shit!"

"Fuck off, you asshole! I do what I want!"

If you were looking for a trigger to make a crazy guy like Renzo go completely ballistic, you couldn't ask for a better one. Now there were four people fighting on the floor, beating the living hell out of each other, and they would have been done pretty soon, as Renzo and Ben were among the best fighters in the Pool Room. But as it's well-known, whoever isn't really good at being tough one-on-one, often compensates with surrounding himself with the same no-good hyenas, unable to stand for themselves on their own, and that's exactly what Billy Bright always did. His friends, several of who were hanging out upstairs, heard about the ongoing fight and came running down with pool sticks to help their buddy out. A very low move you might say, but that's the kind of people they were.

Seeing Billy's reinforcement with the sticks pissed off Renzo even more, and quickly knocking Gangi out, he rushed to Ben's help. Unfortunately, while Renzo was fighting his way back in, one of Bright's guys cracked Ben with a pool stick right on the back of his head and split it wide-open. And now, having an unconscious Ben on the floor and hoping that he wasn't dead, Renzo was left by himself against Billy and a bunch of his guys with pool sticks as weapons. Not a situation you want to find yourself in, unless you have a machine gun hidden behind your back, and since Renzo didn't have a machine gun or any other guns hidden under his jacket, he prepared for the battle of his life, just holding his fists up high.

Once Renzo was involved in a fight, he would become a real killing machine, and you could only feel sorry for the guys who were unfortunate enough to be in his way. And the more of them who would stand in front of him, the angrier he would become. That's what was happening this time in the Pool Room. Renzo was fighting everyone left and right, working his way up the stairs, as he knew that the advantage in any fight belonged to the one who occupied the higher position. Billy Bright's guys were no match for him, and he was easily throwing them down the stairs like the dirt bags they were. But Billy and Gangi soon came back to their senses and now tried to grab Renzo and pull him back down. One of Renzo's famous punches, which knocked down guys bigger and way tougher than Billy and Gangi so many times before, quickly put Billy's buddy back to sleep without dreams when his unconscious body once again hit the stairs.

Renzo was now on top of the stairs, kicking and punching Billy's guys with almost cosmic speed, trying his best to avoid their pool sticks that they were trying to hit him with. One thing he knew for sure: it would be enough to get hit just once, for those bastards to jump him all together, and then he wouldn't be so sure that he could get out of there alive. Meanwhile, Gangi woke up again, took out a big knife that he was always carrying and went through his guys to get Renzo.

"I warn you right now, you try to stab me with that knife, you'll die from it!" Renzo yelled at him, while holding another guy's throat.

Maybe because of a good concussion that Renzo had given him just a couple of minutes ago or maybe because he simply lacked brains, Gangi decided that luck was on his side and swung at Renzo, slightly cutting his jacket.

"That's it, you asked for it, you motherfucker!" Renzo grabbed Gangi's hand, quickly disarmed him and punched him a second time, with all the fury he had.

Seeing one of their leaders lose his weapon so easily and roll down the stairs with blood all over his face, Billy's guys lost their enthusiasm for the fair fist fight and were now trying to hit Renzo with their sticks. That didn't work too well either, and after breaking one of the sticks in two and holding both pieces with sharp ends in front of his face, Renzo said to Billy's attack dogs, circling him like prey, "I know that if you guys jump me, you're gonna fuck me up, and fuck me up badly. But I swear to God, the first one who gets in front of me, will die. I will beat that guy to death, I will tear him apart. Now come on, who wants to be a fuckin hero today? Huh? Who wants to die first?"

Was it the look on his face that left them doubtless of his intentions to kill one of them that day, was it his reputation that made them intimidated of him, even though technically he was outnumbered almost fifteen-to-one? Whatever it was, no one felt brave enough to try his luck. Renzo quickly realized that this was his chance and quickly got away through the back entrance. When he drove up to the front to see what had happened to Ben, Renzo saw he was gone! No trace of him at all, even within a few blocks radius of the Pool Room. Renzo had no choice but to drive back to 85th St. and hopefully find him there.

There was shouting from the top floor of the apartment building on the corner that Ben's girl lived in; her father was saying he had Ben upstairs with a towel on top of his head to try and control the bleeding. Renzo ran up the stairs as fast as he could to find Ben covered in fresh blood, still pouring out of him like a broken water pipe.

"Oh, buddy, we gotta get you to the hospital, and fast!" Renzo helped him down the stairs to his car, opened the passenger's door for Ben and gave him a fresh towel from the back seat, fortunately forgotten there after Renzo's workout that day.

"No, I'm OK," Ben muttered. "Don't worry about it."

"OK my ass!" Renzo shook his head, wondering if the whole former feud between the two guys was actually worth almost dying for, but he didn't say anything. The wiseguy code (even for a very young wiseguy) clearly stated that if your friend needed you there, you went, no matter what time of day, no matter where he was, no matter what he had done. No questions asked, you just went and helped him out, because one day he'd do the same for you.

Renzo drove as fast as he could, trying to get Ben to Coney Island Hospital before bleeding to death, but having his head cracked open didn't really seem to faze Ben as much as it did Renzo.

"You know, I think I'm not gonna go to the hospital," Ben said. "I think I'd better go see my girlfriend."

"What?!" Renzo thought that the concussion was probably serious if Ben started saying crazy things like what he just said. "You aren't going anywhere! Look at your head, you're bleeding like a pig! You need stitches right away!"

"Fuck the stitches, I want to see my girlfriend." Even though he was mumbling, Ben sounded pretty determined.

"Well, too fuckin bad for you. This is not really your decision to make. I'm driving the car, so just sit back and shut up."

"OK."

Ben adjusted his seat down and a little more to the back, so he was almost lying down now. Renzo kept driving on Ocean Parkway, singing along with the radio to try and keep both of them calm, when suddenly in the rearview mirror he saw something rolling in the street.

"What the hell was that? A deer? Did you see that?"

Renzo turned to Ben, but all he saw was the opened door and an empty passenger's seat.

"That fuckin idiot!!!"

Renzo jammed his brakes as hard as he could and made a wide U-turn, trying to catch up with his nutty friend. But when he reached the spot where Ben had jumped out, there was nobody in sight. Renzo kept driving around the area, calling his buddy's name, looking for any traces, but there was nothing. Ben simply disappeared into the night. *Well, what else can I do?* Renzo thought, turning his car toward home. *He's gone. I guess I'll just have to look for this nut tomorrow.*

The next day Renzo went to see Ben's parents to see if they had heard any news about their son. And that's where he found Ben himself, simply smiling at him and pointing to his head, which at that point resembled Frankenstein's a lot—that's how many stitches crossed his skull. It turned out he did go to see his girlfriend right after jumping out of Renzo's car, and it was her who took him to the hospital right away. Renzo didn't know if he should laugh or cry because of how insane his friend was. And for the first time he started asking himself, was it him who attracted all the psychos, or was it just bad luck? But no matter how crazy all his friends were, Renzo loved them all like brothers and treated them the same way. *You go—I go*. And that's what always made them so invincible.

Just like most of the other "family" members, I have never had any respect for "rats." What, as soon as the feds bust your ass, you start squealing like a little girl, trying to cut down your sentence? Or even better… you go under a witness protection program to later become a "reality star" on the History channel, talking with a funny voice about how bad your former buddies were? Well, you deserve to have your throat slit, that's what your sorry ass deserves. There are no former buddies in the family, that's what's supposed to keep it strong, and you go and break your oath just like that? You're not a tough guy, you're not a wiseguy, you're just a rat, as simple as that.

The funniest thing was that he had his ass busted for drunk driving! It wasn't a police bust, no federal investigation—they had nothing on him, nothing! How stupid was that? I bet that poor cop never suspected that night that the drunk driver, who he had just arrested, would start spilling his guts like he was on a fucking talk show! Yep, that was my "good buddy" Frank, who I had knocked out three times in the Pool Room. Even though the guy who he ratted out was a major asshole himself, it still wasn't an excuse. That's not what an associate of a family did. And they had even almost been best buddies at some point, Frank and Tommy, who thanks to Frank got a life sentence. Not that he didn't deserve it for killing almost sixty people and cutting them up…

That was the truth, they were at some point almost best buddies, Frank and Tommy, known as Tommy Karate for his love of martial arts, which was so strong that his teenage years were spent in Japan studying it with one of the most celebrated and deadliest teachers in the world. At one point he even grew his hair down to his shoulders to resemble his long-time idol, Bruce Lee. Tommy's skills in martial arts were his compensation for his high-pitched voice, for which he was often bullied in high school and picked on by his buddies. Even Frank would say that he can't figure out who Tommy sounded more like: Mickey or Minnie Mouse.

However, his high, almost feminine voice, didn't stop him from making quite a career in the Brooklyn mob family. In the course of several years of good service as a soldier—including the speculated killing of Wilfred "Willie Boy" Johnson as a favor to the Gambino crime boss, John Gotti, who had just found out that his one-time close friend Johnson turned out to be a government informant since 1966—Tommy was offered the position of a made man, which he more than gladly accepted. But that position didn't do him any good; on the contrary, that kind of promotion only drove his already quite active sadistic and abnormal behavior to a completely new level.

Of course, the Italian mafia is not the Catholic Church, those guys kill people. But unlike some Chicago gangs or Colombian drug dealers, who are technically just a bunch of armed petty criminals, Italian mobsters form almost a state within a state with their own rules and regulations, with their highly structured hierarchy and very strict laws and traditions. They don't just walk around looking for somebody to shoot; just the opposite: murder, drug dealing and prostitution are considered "dirty" business among those dons in tailored suites, and they try to stay away from it as much as they can, settling on minor misdemeanors like illegal gambling, which in many cases is actually much more of a profitable source of income than dealing drugs. They rarely kill people without having a really good reason for it, like somebody turning out to be a rat or being a threat to the boss of the family. Tommy, in his time, just enjoyed killing them for the "fun" of it.

He wasn't just your average wiseguy, Tommy was a serial killer, that's what it looked like to me. First of all he became a drug dealer, which was a big no-no in the "family" to begin with, but listen to this: he would steal drugs from his "business partners" from the Middle East and South America, then he would cut them ("business partners") up and resell their drugs for his own profit. How sick was that?

And his pet dog, Frank, would help him out in all this. When the cops started digging, they found Tommy's little personal cemetery in Staten Island, where he had buried all those bodies, sometimes in suitcases, sometimes wrapped in plastic and decapitated so it would be impossible to identify them without the dental records.

He was a sick man, I don't know how else you would explain a guy who killed another guy, then put that guy's body in the bathtub, got undressed, put the water on, got in the same bathtub and cut the body up, keeping the water running so it would wash all the blood right away. He was a psychopath. I don't really see a normal person doing something like that without even blinking an eye. Tommy worked on those bodies like a fuckin brain surgeon. He even carried his own set of instruments with him all the time, just in case he needed to cut somebody up. He was really good at it. But you haven't heard the most fucked-up part yet: he killed his friend Frank's girlfriend and made Frank cut her up! My sincerest apologies if you just threw up.

His girl's name was Phyllis, and she was drop dead gorgeous. She reminded me of Cindy Crawford a little bit, what a doll! Too bad she was on heavy drugs, which her boyfriend, Frank, was more than happy to supply her with as long as she would put out, you know. Tommy's wife, Celeste, got caught up in the same shit, and while Tommy kept telling her to stay away from Phyllis, as he thought of Phyllis as a bad influence, Celeste didn't really care. She just wanted to party…

Sad story, she was a very, very beautiful girl as well, but one night, when all four of them were partying and carrying on, Celeste overdosed and died. Tommy was devastated, he decided that it was all Phyllis's fault and shot her, right there, in the bed. And after that he made Frank cut her up. You would think he wouldn't be able to cut up his own girlfriend. Well, Frank knew Tommy too well—it was either he cut her up, or being shot and cut up by Tommy himself. Frank didn't want to die, that's all… end of story.

They say Tommy killed over sixty people, but they could only prove six with the help of Frank, who said that he couldn't live with that kind of guilt anymore and wanted to start a new life. They almost put Tommy on death row, but somehow to his luck the jury decided that a life sentence would be enough for him. Frank got away with his witness protection thing. I guess he's somewhere far, far away from New York now, living his new life… They deserved each other, Frank and Tommy, and they deserved what they both got. It's one thing to shoot some asshole who wanted to kill your boss, and another thing to keep their wedding bands as souvenirs in your fuckin apartment! That's just not normal! And no wiseguy would ever kill a woman, that's a long time-honored law, and you don't go and break it like that! It's very low, it's very sick, and it's a good thing they didn't get away with that because eventually they would have paid for it.

Chapter 4

"The Ultimate Killing Machine"

Renzo, remarkable as he was in his own crazy way, probably had that little incident in the Pool Room to thank for attracting a lot of the very heavy duty wiseguys' admiration and attention. Probably another factor in gaining the Bensonhurst goodfellas' trust was Renzo's father's close friendship with one of the bosses of the family, Rocco. Rocco loved Renzo's father, Frank, for his loyalty, for being a smartass at times and for his Sinatra voice. One time Frank even got to sing in front of his idol in one of the Manhattan hot spots, and even though he was completely freaked out, he did a great job, even earning a compliment from Sinatra himself, "Good job, kid!"

Every Thursday those underground rulers of Brooklyn, the unspoken presidents of the borough, gathered in one of the restaurants owned by their close friends and discussed their next move, involving businesses and probably the fate of the whole neighborhood, as no politician had more power than they did. After all, if you had to choose who you should fear more, a politician or a wiseguy, you'd probably take into consideration that the politician won't shoot you in the head and drop your body somewhere in the ocean if you don't follow his lead.

But they weren't really bad guys; thanks to them the neighborhood was under control and was always protected from anybody who would try to flex their muscles in the wrong territory. Yes, a lot of business owners had to pay their "bills" on time, but they slept well at night knowing that if somebody decided to muscle in, they had a very powerful force protecting them better than any police or security guards could.

You wouldn't always go to the police back then: choosing a cop to trust your secrets or to rat somebody out to was like playing Russian roulette—you never knew if they were being paid under the table by the same mobster who you were trying to report. And the history proves that, just like in the case of that unfortunate captain of the Gambino mob family Edward "Eddie" Lino, whose murder was ordered by Anthony "Gaspipe" Casso as a favor to the Genovese crime family boss, Vincent "Chin" Gigante.

Gigante wasn't too happy with the growing power of the rival mob family and wanted once and for all to show everyone who owned the neighborhood. He did so by utilizing two corrupt NYPD detectives, Louis Eppolito and Stephen Caracappa, both of whom had been working for the mobsters for a long time, making hundreds of thousands of untaxable dollars in bribes and payments for murder contracts. One of those contracts was on Lino, who had no idea that the unmarked police car, which had just pulled his Mercedes over, would be the last thing he would see in his life. Eppolito and Caracappa shot Eddie Lino nine times, leaving him no chance for survival. You probably understand why the business owners preferred mobsters to the police: at least the mobsters weren't hiding their real faces.

Those guys knew what they were doing, but when it would come to a really big job, they needed the fastest getaway driver around. And here's when Renzo's quite astonishing driving record came to their attention. I mean who else could steal more than forty cars by the age of seventeen and not be caught once? They asked themselves this question and pretty soon made Renzo their official getaway driver. Rocco, who was not only good friends with Renzo's father, Frank, but who was also Renzo's godfather, took the young man under his wing right away and decided to teach him whatever he knew himself. Rocco loved him like a son, and Renzo was really lucky because to be honest he attracted trouble like a magnet. Getting into fights with the sons of wiseguys was his everyday entertainment, and Rocco quickly became tired of cleaning up Renzo's messes.

"What am I gonna do with you?" Rocco would say in place of their usual morning greetings.

"It's not really my fault, Rocco, they were disrespectful." Renzo's doe eyes seemed to work their magic even on a hardcore mob boss.

"You're lucky that you have a pretty face. You're gonna be a perfect front man one day. With those innocent eyes, nobody will ever believe what you're capable of."

Even though Renzo did have a pretty short fuse, he would only get aggressive with those who really deserved it. He wasn't a blood-thirsty maniac, killing people just for fun like a lot of the "soldiers" in the family. He was happy enough just driving a car, playing catch with the feds on his tail, every time losing them easily to the amazement of his passengers. All the bosses were very happy with their choice: to this day, Renzo hasn't been caught once by the police, nor by federal agents. He was the perfect driver, with years of experience and ambition to make him the best of the best.

They were proud young men, proud of their origin, proud of their accomplishments and their circle. Pride plays a very important role in Italian-American society: whatever they do, they mostly do from their national pride. I mean, have you ever seen an Italian-American who isn't proud of his roots? No. It's very understandable though, they have one of the best cuisines in the world, their language is simply awesome, they live till one hundred years old (if they don't get shot or stabbed by a rival mobster), and they do all this while drinking like crazy, smoking and carrying on like there's no tomorrow. And even all this put aside, they descend from the great Romans, who conquered half of the world! Who in their right mind wouldn't be jealous of them?

All this explains why they just *had to* start a fight if someone disrespected them. Disrespect is a big and very often used word among Italian-American society.

If you talk to someone's wife or girl in a flirty way—it's disrespectful, and you most likely will get a beating. If you don't treat the elderly politely—it's also disrespectful, and you will get a beating (in most cases from the elderly themselves, as those nutty Italians are able to kick your ass till they're ninety). If someone important holds a big dinner like a Birthday party, a child's Christening or a wedding and you don't show up for whatever reason—it's disrespectful, and depending on your status you will get the silent treatment for a certain period of time, a serious sit down or a beating (from the important person's people because important people themselves are too busy shooting and burying bodies to deal with other important people). So it's not really those kids' fault, they were simply raised like that, with all those principles injected directly into their blood stream from their mother's milk. They couldn't help it, it was who they were and it was their lifestyle, and if you don't like it, well, guess what, you'll get a beating!

A lot of no-good deeds were driven by that Italian pride, which the following story is just another example. Caroline was a very pretty girl, one of the most popular ones in the neighborhood, and Renzo's friend Anthony was crazy in love with her. But Anthony was a little overweight, a little too clumsy and seemed to lose his speech around any kind of female every single time. He tried really hard to attract Caroline's attention, but all he got were jokes and condescending permission to drive her and her girlfriends to whatever place they wished to go. Finally, when he got tired of being pushed around (as any other proud Italian would get sooner or later), he did something that Caroline and her girlfriends wouldn't forget for quite a long time.

It was a hot summer day, and Anthony and Renzo just picked up Caroline and two of her girlfriends at their house to drive them to the movie theatre. A day ago she clearly told Anthony in front of the same girlfriends that they could only be friends and he couldn't really count on anything serious with her, so needless to say, Anthony was not in the best mood. He was driving his "open" car in dead silence, while the girls in the back seat, all dolled up for the movies, were enjoying the sun, giggling and happily discussing the shopping they just had done and the movie they were going to see.

Even Renzo had no idea what his friend had on his mind, which was the following master plan that came to life as soon as he saw an open fire hydrant, gushing water out to the joy of all the kids on the block. Without even blinking an eye, Anthony drove right next to it, made sure that all the doors were locked and put his car in park. Within seconds the screaming girls got soaking wet, their dresses and fancy hair-do's ruined thanks to Anthony, who had the most satisfied grin on his face. He didn't seem to care that his car was going to be ruined; in his mind, it was totally worth it. Renzo was cracking up in the front seat, picking up his legs from the water filling up the car with a cosmic speed. All the people on the block were laughing their asses off, and the only ones who didn't seem to share in the fun that everybody was having were Caroline and her girlfriends.

"Anthony, you idiot, what the hell did you do?!" Caroline screamed at him.

"Oh, please! Whatcha gonna do now, break up with me?" Probably for the first time Anthony felt confident in Caroline's presence. A soaked girl with running make up didn't intimidate him.

After enjoying his victorious moment of glory for another several minutes, Anthony at last drove away from the fire hydrant. When he finally stopped the car and opened the door, the water gushed out of it like from a bathtub. Renzo was dying laughing, and the girls didn't speak to Anthony for a good several months after that incident. They learned their lesson the hard way: even if you're a hot girl, you're not safe around an Italian guy with hurt pride.

A lot of times they were just trying to prove to themselves and the others how cool they were, although the way those young twenty-year-old kids were going about it would make a regular non-Italian person's hair stand up. And not only bad things would come out of their pride. For example this one time they decided to catch a serial killer before the police could…

The killer's name was David Berkowitz, also known as The .44 Caliber Killer or The Son of Sam, responsible for at least six dead and seven wounded, and also, as it has been stated from the diaries found in his apartment in Yonkers, about 1400 arsons throughout the whole of New York. He was supposedly a schizophrenic or some satanic cult observer, and he had an obvious soft spot for beautiful girls. Berkowitz first started shooting his victims in 1976, and his signature weapon of choice was a .44 caliber revolver. He shot his victims mostly late at night, sneaking up on them in their parked cars, where they were making out (if it was a couple) or discussing the movie they had just seen (if it were two girls). As Berkowitz later explained in one of the letters that he sent to the police, "Queens girls were the prettiest," and that's why most of the killings took place in that neighborhood, with victims all being long-haired pretty brunettes. That last fact caused such a panic among the female population of New York that hair salons couldn't manage the traffic of women all asking for their long dark hair to be cut or dyed.

After several more killings and fruitless efforts by the police to identify or catch Berkowitz, Renzo and his friends decided to take law enforcement into their own hands. They started going in their cars to the "hot spots" where the killer could have appeared and waiting for him in the dark with loaded guns ready to fire. I guess he can consider himself lucky that they didn't catch him before the police, as he would have most certainly been killed, and his body would have been found days later swimming with the fish.

But Renzo was very, very close to it: Berkowitz's last shooting surprisingly took place in the Bath area of Brooklyn instead of the usual Queens, and this time he was very sloppy, leaving a lot of witnesses behind due to the bright light of the full moon. Most of the witnesses later positively identified both him and his car. Later in the 60th precinct in Coney Island, Brooklyn, it took less than thirty minutes for Berkowitz to confess to all the killings. He explained that his neighbor's dog, a chocolate mix lab, was making him kill people, as "it was possessed by an ancient demon demanding blood of young, beautiful women." If he had said something like that to Renzo and his friends, they would have probably fallen on the floor laughing their asses off before killing the guy. But anyway, Berkowitz was sentenced to several consecutive first degree murder charges and will be able to come out of jail in about 150 years from now.

Pride was the reason why they wanted to affirm their position within their circles, to flex their muscles and to create their future reputation. But sometimes, when somebody who they were supposed to respect was disrespecting them… well, you already know, they would get a beating. One such guy was Tomasso, and he was a very heavy duty wiseguy. Frank, Renzo's father, was making a sign for Tomasso's business, and just like in most cases with those wiseguys (who were used to never being charged for anything, assuming that everyone should be happy to give them stuff for free), Tomasso refused to pay. But Frank didn't take anybody's shit; whether it was a wiseguy or the President of the United States, his motto was, "You don't pay for the sign—the sign comes down, period." He didn't care who his client was, he was tougher than nails and would kick anybody's ass, just give him a reason!

So just like in any other case with a payment not received, Frank sent Renzo to take the sign down in the middle of the night; you couldn't do it during the day as the owner had the right to call the police, who would most certainly tell them to go to court with this civil case. The next day Tomasso, furious, stormed into Frank's sign shop, shaking his fists and demanding an explanation. Frank, calm as a rock, just looked at Tomasso while continuing to work on his current project.

"I told you," Frank said, "you don't pay the bill by Monday, I'll take the sign down. I don't do charity work here, I have a family to feed."

"Do you know who I am?"

"Don't you know who you are?" Frank's sarcastic reply cracked up Renzo and several workers in the shop, and that's what sent Tomasso absolutely ballistic.

"Do you want to fuck with me? I'll fuckin kill you right here and—" Frank's knockout punch didn't let Tomasso finish his thought and sent him right into the opposite wall.

"Go ahead," Frank said, cleaning his hand with a towel, still calm as calm could be. "I would like to see you try."

Infuriated, Tomasso, who was a pretty big guy, couldn't take the thought of being humiliated in front of all the shop workers by a much shorter Frank, so he jumped right back on him, trying to avenge himself. Here they were, rolling on the floor, beating the shit out of each other, and here's Renzo, who didn't like anybody threatening and especially jumping on his father in front of him. He grabbed one of the metallic pipes that he had been welding for one of the signs and started smashing it on Tomasso's head and back. Now taking into consideration that Renzo was a healthy young twenty-year-old man with a lot of energy, who was working out on a daily basis, the impact of his hits, combined with Frank's deadly punches, quickly made Tomasso beg for help.

"Get your fuckin kid off me!!! He's gonna crack my fuckin head!!!"

According to Frank's personal gentleman's code, he didn't like to continue punching a guy who was waving a white flag, so he just calmly got off of him and told his son to leave Tomasso alone.

"Don't waste your energy on this asshole, son. He got what he deserved."

"I'll be back, do you hear me?"

"Anytime you want to get the next beating, you are always more than welcome."

Bleeding from his nose and his left eye, Tomasso walked out the shop, giving Frank and Renzo a last dirty look. Frank just shrugged and went back to work like nothing had ever happened. Sneaky Renzo, meanwhile, picked up a big diamond ring, which Tomasso had lost from his pinky during the fight, and put it in his pocket. The next day he got a call from his godfather, Rocco.

"I don't care what you did to the guy, it's all straightened out. Just bring me back the ring."

Renzo started laughing. "How did you know I had it?"

"Kid, unfortunately I know you too well by now. Just bring it back, before I personally kick your ass!"

The whole episode was soon "forgotten" by Tomasso, but since then, all the other wiseguys knew quite well that Frank's signs have to be paid for.

You couldn't be an Italian guy from Bensonhurst if you couldn't kick some ass. They always fought, and they fought a lot. They fought because they got drunk and stupid, they fought because somebody disrespected them, they fought because their boss told them to fight, they fought because they were hot-blooded Italians and they just liked it. They've fought since they were little boys, and they'll keep doing it until they die. It's kind of a lifestyle, just like Samurai swords for Japanese people or corrida for Spanish. That Southern, testosterone-inflated DNA wouldn't leave them alone, and it will keep locking their hands into fists at every possible opportunity. They all know that, they all have learned to live with it and frankly speaking, they are kind of proud of it.

That's quite understandable: it's much more interesting to discuss who gave whom a beating last night than to talk about the stock market or the current situation in the Middle East. They know they can't change the latter, however, they can always put in their place the unfortunate individual who was stupid enough to somehow piss them off (even though it's not too hard to do so). The biggest bragging right in that tight Italian-American community of Brooklyn is being able to say you went through an entire fight without getting your face touched. You can get shot, you can suffer from a couple of broken bones, but if you can manage to never get a split lip in a good showdown, then you're considered a really tough guy. Renzo is very proud that he can call himself that type of guy. But the road to becoming an almost invincible fighter was not that easy even for him.

I first got into martial arts in my early twenties. And to tell you the truth, I got my ass kicked every single time during the first couple of years. My trainer's name was Mike, he was a real nut and the toughest guy I've ever seen in the ring, and when we would spar he would beat the crap out of me! He had his own politics concerning the rules: no gloves, no protective head or body gear, no bullshit as he would call it. We were literary fist fighting each other in that ring, until somebody would get his nose broken or his ribs cracked.

It was the toughest workout you can possibly think of—Mike was making us ready for actual street fights. And since I've always had that perfectionist mentality, I just had to become the best of the best. I couldn't settle for second place, no way! So I started working my ass off, learning his techniques and his speed to make sure that with time I could actually match him in his skills, and after that, beat him up. Well, long story short, after a couple of years, after several broken ribs, cracked hand bones, a split eyebrow and having my nose broken twice, I finally did. After that one time that I beat the shit out of Mike, he said to me, "Renzo, that's it, I'm not sparring you no more!"

It was the best compliment he could have ever possibly given me.

The place itself where we were training was a whole separate story itself. It was an apartment in Starrett City with concrete walls, in the blackest neighborhood that you could ever find! There were always gangs hanging out in the area, and we were the only white guys there. They didn't touch us, but when they saw me for the first time they told me, "Man, you must have really big balls coming here!"

I just smirked and walked right by them. All gangs are the same, they're like a pack of dogs and they can smell your fear. And if you show them that you have no fear at all, they will respect you and leave you alone. As those guys did after that single encounter. They never touched me or my friends… if they did, they would have had their asses kicked anyway—I mean, after beating up almost fifteen guys in the Pool Room almost single-handedly, those guys wouldn't have been a problem for me and my buddies. I think they knew that.

There were actually four of us: my trainer Mike, his friend Paul, my buddy Jim and me. Aside from being a trainer, Mike also worked for the courts. He was the best of the best when it came to the polygraph and had his own company, which was in very high demand. So he would always bring all those court officers, firefighters and cops who wanted to train, and they would spar with us. It's funny if you think that we had our own private fight club and the law enforcement guys were voluntarily coming down to get a beating from us guys who were, let's say, "on the other side of the tracks." Some politicians even joined the club too!

They were great guys though, I made a lot of friends with them and still have all kinds of shields that get me out of tickets and drunk driving arrests. I mean, who in their right mind would let go of a man who was almost making donuts at the turn of a busy intersection, cut off an unmarked police car, and when they pulled him over and asked, "Sir, do you know why I pulled you over tonight?" he answered, "Yeah, you cut me off!"

"I cut you off?!"

"Yeah!!!"

My business partner Ralph, who was with me in the car, was already making arrangements in his mind about where he was going to get money to bail me out of jail and where he should leave my car. They saw my wallet with all those shields and had to let me go with one condition that Ralph would drive. It's funny, he got sober right away and was talking to them like a frigging cadet in a police academy.

"Have you been drinking tonight, sir?"

"Absolutely not, sir!"

"Can you drive his car?"

"Absolutely yes, sir!"

I was dying laughing my ass off!

But going back to our training: one time Mike brought this guy in, his name was Fred, a really tough guy and a former semi pro boxer! When we sparred and he caught me in the stomach, I felt like I was gonna die, but I never showed it. He respected my heart and determination. So we were sparring, working out, having a great time, and during the break he started telling us about himself; you know, we liked getting to know each other, we were like one big crazy family there… So here he went, saying that he used to live far, far upstate New York and he had a farm there, with cows, sheep and chickens, all kinds of animals.

And then he said, “Do you know that a sheep’s vagina is the closest to a woman’s?”

He didn’t say that he had fucked a sheep or anything, he just mentioned it as a scientific fact or whatever. But I wasn’t going to get a better chance to pick it up and roll with it! So I said (with a very serious face), “Wait a minute. So you’re saying that you eat with the sheep, you sleep with the sheep, you have sex with the sheep… are there any side effects?”

And I answered myself as if I was him but made my voice sound like a sheep, “Naaaaaah!”

The guys were dying! They were all cracking up, even Fred himself! But I kept going on and on with it, even when we went back to practicing. From time to time, I talked in my “sheep” voice, “Freeeed! Fuuuck meeee! Freeeed!!!”

The guys were all dying laughing. Only Mike kept trying to keep order, but it didn’t work too well. As soon as I find something that bothers you, I’ll keep doing it. And if you show me that it bothers you and ask me to stop, I’ll do it a hundred times more! That guy Fred never came back after that time, but all the guys still remember my crazy joke. We still do it from time to time.

Mike was indeed bringing remarkable people to his gym, and one of those remarkable people was the first legally blind governor of New York, David Paterson. Even though Paterson wasn't a governor yet, he was already in office and soon became a good friend of Renzo's trainer, Mike. Renzo didn't even know back then who the guy was, probably because he wasn't really into politics; he was much more interested in the other "governors" and "mayors" of Bensonhurst, who back then probably had more power than the real ones.

Renzo was more than happy to try all the new stuff that Mike was throwing at him. Mike made the workout as diverse and unpredictable as he possibly could, making every sparring match, every "one-on-one," feel as if it was a real street fight. One time Mike had in mind a new routine, a sensitivity training exercise, where two fighters locked hands without disengaging while trying to strike each other with their free hand. The hardest part of the exercise was that you literally had to be in each other's face, a hand's distance away, and you couldn't escape the punches by jumping away. The only thing you could do was pull your body back or twist your body away. Taking into consideration that Paterson could only see shadows and silhouettes, making it very tough for him to fight, he was doing fantastic, making fast progress and even keeping up with Renzo.

Dave had very fast hands and was very aggressive. It was a very tough exercise, and we were kicking the crap out of each other! And to do this exercise properly, you actually had to be blindfolded, but we didn't want to be rude to Paterson. If you're blindfolded, it's even harder to fight, because you had to literally sense your opponent's aggressive moves and respond to them quickly. I'm not one hundred percent sure, but I think Mike actually blindfolded me at some point… It really taught you how to have keen senses, like a good attack dog! But you couldn't really hurt anyone during this drill… I mean, you couldn't jump back and you couldn't really strike them, all you could do was roll off your opponent's hands. And there's no way that you could strike anyone hard enough to do any real damage from that distance. It's not really a sparring exercise, it just improved your intuition during a fight.

After the workout Renzo and David shook hands and decided to keep working out together whenever they both had time. Mike is still good friends with David Paterson, and they quite often get together and remember the good old times in Renzo's private gym.

My father and I got this new shop on Coney Island Ave, and since I wasn't a teenager anymore but a grown man in my late twenties, he let me do whatever I wanted with it. It was huge, two stories high, and I decided to leave the sign shop on the first floor and to make my own playground on the second. I wanted my own Pool Room but without all that gang-related bullshit, you know? So we put a bar and a pool table in one room and made a huge gym out of the second one. We had everything there: dumbbells, weights, a heavy bag, a small boxing ring; you name it, we had it. And so started my own Pool Room era, and it later became a preparation room for myself and my buddies before we would hit the road to party in the craziest City clubs, like Studio 54 and Red Parrot.

A new era is a pretty big deal. It was our declaration of independence, our own private club, so we had to celebrate it; and we did so almost like other people celebrate New Year's. And here's when Paul bought Quaaludes, his drug of choice. Not too bad for the seventies, when people were doing just about everything they could possibly find. We had a couple of drinks, we played some pool, then Paul got them out and invited us to be his guests. Now when it comes to a party, I'm pretty much up for anything, even though I don't really feel any effect from drugs. So I did it, just socially, in order not to offend my friends and not to be a pussy.

So all four of us took them, and while we were waiting for them to kick in, we decided to hang out in the gym and work out a little. And then, almost simultaneously, all three of them got hit! They started talking funny, walking really slowly and acting like complete retards. Watching them try to act normal when they all were absolutely fucked-up—I just sat on the floor crying, that's how hard I was laughing! Jim got hit the hardest though and started walking very slowly in circles through the room, looking at the walls and us as if he didn't realize where the fuck he was and who all these people were. We were flipping out laughing at him! But Paul decided to be the funny guy and swung the heavy bag at Jim, who was walking right next to it. The funniest part was that the heavy bag didn't hit him the first time, it just flew right behind him without him even realizing what was going on. And here I called out his name so he would look at it and duck, but his reaction time was so slow because of the Ludes that he just turned his head to me like in a slow-motion movie and said really slowly, "Whaaaaht?"

The fuckin heavy bag picked him up right off his legs and threw him across the room. It was one of the funniest things I've ever seen!

We knew how to party, but we also knew how to work hard. Mike never let us just goof around, but even when he was in training mode, he was a real beast! And what Mike believed in was that the more different people you spar, the better fighter you become, as you learn how to react to every possible unpredictable situation. He was absolutely right, and thanks to him I've never had my ass kicked. So I guess his theory worked. Mike also believed in constant improvement of your skills; his motto was "The only person you compete against is you a day ago." He wanted us to always beat our own records, to learn something new, to make our muscles stronger, to find a weak part of our bodies and make it stronger than ever. He wanted us to be his own champions, so he started to bring real boxers to our training sessions and made us spar with them.

One time he brought in this guy Ernesto. He was a really tough court officer, and Mike wanted me to spar him. I didn't care if he was an ex-golden gloves boxer; when you start thinking that someone is better than you just because they're some kind of a professional fighter, that's when you lose. Ernesto looked me up and down, and Mike told him to hit me in the stomach with all his strength. Ernesto wound up and punched me really hard. I didn't show any reaction. He looked at me and said, "Let me try that again!" He gave it his best shot, and I didn't flinch again.

He looked at my instructor and said, "I ain't sparring this guy… no fuckin way!"

"He's the craziest kid I've ever trained," Mike said. "If he keeps going like this, nobody will want to spar him anymore!"

I just laughed. It was nice of him to say that. My dad could be finally proud of his son, who had just completed the transformation from a shy momma's boy into the ultimate killing machine. I'm not so sure if it was a good thing though…

Chapter 5

"The Seventies Era"

"Never rat on your friends and always keep your mouth shut."

(R. De Niro as Jimmy Conway)

The seventies were actively taking over, and Renzo and his friends were enjoying every single day of the party era. How could you not enjoy it when you were making good money, had impressive connections and were handsome as hell? They were always more than welcome in the hottest City spots, such as Studio 54 and years later The Red Parrot. They were always among the best dressed and good-looking young men waiting at the doors of those two hottest hangouts—well, actually they never even had to wait too long in line: the managers knew them, or knew of them and who they were associated with, and easily granted them access to the VIP area with no questions asked.

One time, while they were enjoying their drinks behind the red ropes at the Red Parrot, Eddie Murphy himself, the coolest actor of that time, accompanied by the two gorgeous girls on his arm, walked in. After exchanging handshakes with Renzo and his crew, Murphy settled down next to them and pretty soon invited them to join his little "party," which meant openly doing blow off the table, where everyone in the club was able to see them. They didn't care, it was the disco era and everybody was doing it. You would actually stand out if you didn't do it, so nobody thought of it as something shocking or obscene.

As a matter of fact, cocaine at that time was so popular that clubbers and some lawyers and stock market brokers (who were probably the majority of the consumers) carried little bottles filled with the white powder and tiny spoons attached to them for convenient use. Some girls even wore them hanging from their necks like a piece of jewelry… now how sick was that? It gets even better: back in the days of Studio 54, they had a huge prop of a half-moon descend from the ceiling in the middle of the night with a pretty girl sitting on it, and below it was a big coke spoon. It was an unspoken signal for all the people on the dance floor to take another hit from their little bottles and spoons, even though they were already wired up so much that sweat was streaming down their faces as if they were dancing in the rain.

The coolest thing about Studio 54 was that you could get in just because you looked good. The crazy owner, Steve Rubell, stood by the door himself and picked the lucky ones to let inside his chaotic disco heaven, and if you met his standards, you had a chance to party with famous actors, politicians, artists, musicians—you name it, Steve had it. You could be a broke waiter trying to make it in New York City, but once you were admitted to this club, you were one of the chosen ones, you could completely forget your miserable daytime life and just have fun, partying like there's no tomorrow. Of course, people were overdosing right there on the dance floor, but who's going to say that it wasn't the perfect way for them to possibly die?

Renzo was never into drugs, but it was a coke era and he was a social user, despite the fact that he didn't really feel any effect of the drug himself. He just cracked a little laughter every time one of his friends would overdo it and get cotton mouthed. Later he would rip on that friend in front of everybody, telling the story of that poor guy acting like a retard in all the detail he could remember. You couldn't use drugs and be safe around Renzo. Having a fantastic memory, he would recall every stupid thing you did or said and would keep tearing you a second asshole until someone new would outdo you with something even more retarded—then Renzo would switch his attention to his next victim.

But not all of Renzo's clubbing experiences ended up being so amusing. If you're from New York, you have probably heard of a guy named Sammy "The Bull" Gravano, a former underboss of the Gambino crime family turned federal witness and a big construction businessman. Aside from leading his business and taking care of his "family," Gravano also owned a night club in Brooklyn called The Plaza Suite, which was the equivalent to Studio 54 in the City, with people waiting in line for more than an hour to get in. Maybe because of their fascination with the mob, maybe because of the high-profile artists of the time playing there, such as Chubby Checker and the Four Tops, but people were dying to get in, sometimes literally.

One of those “dying to get in” people was Frank Fiala, a very prosperous businessman and an even more prosperous drug dealer. Mr. Fiala was pretty much used to getting whatever he wanted, either by buying it or killing for it, and this time he wanted The Plaza Suite. Fiala offered Sammy Gravano a million dollars for the club, which Sammy the Bull valued only at $200,000. So without hesitating too long, Gravano accepted the offer. However, before the transaction was complete, Fiala had already started acting as if he owned the place, a fact that very much pissed Gravano off.

The straw that broke the camel’s (or shall we say, the Bull’s) back was the day Fiala settled in to Gravano’s private office and started his own renovations there. When the spitfire Sammy the Bull, followed by his right-hand man, Garafola, stormed into the office demanding an explanation from Fiala, the latter pulled an Uzi from under the table and only laughed in their faces.

“Sit down,” Fiala told them. “You fucking greaseballs, you do things my way.”

No one ever spoke to Sammy Gravano this way before, and whoever had tried to, ended up dead and missing. Fiala was smart (or cowardly) enough not to kill the two men right in his office, however, but by pulling such a stunt, he had just scorned the “made man” and decided his fate once and for all.

Renzo and his friends were waiting in line to get into The Plaza Suite. They had no idea about what had happened inside just a couple of hours ago. They were laughing, talking about their day, their job and their girls, when Frank Fiala and his entourage made their exit. Then all of a sudden they saw Gravano, who seemed to appear out of nowhere right behind Fiala. Gravano loudly asked him, "Hey, Frank, how you doing?"

As soon as Fiala turned around to see the guy he had just been threatening with a gun not too long ago, one of Gravano's guys shot Fiala in the back of his head. Then, accompanied by the screams of the quickly-dispersing crowd, Fiala's executioner stood over his dead body and fired a shot into each of his eyes. Renzo knew that the dead guy had probably done something very wrong when Sammy the Bull walked over to the body and spit on it. Later, when the police arrived to interrogate the witnesses, Renzo only smiled at them and said that neither he, nor his buddies, had seen anybody. It had been very dark and all they knew was that someone had shot somebody and everybody had run. The police had no reason not to believe Renzo's doe eyes for the millionth time, and even though some other witnesses were more descriptive in their testimony, Gravano himself made sure that the case was in the safe hands of the mafia's good buddy, the lead NYPD homicide detective, Louis Eppolito, who for as little as $5000 soon stated that the investigation yielded no leads.

The new era didn't only bring financial independence and parties at the hottest city spots; it also brought a new circle Renzo soon became a part of, consisting of even nuttier friends, who had the dangerously close attention of law enforcement. Renzo didn't care though, when you're young and are not afraid to die, you become a pretty scary fella to mess with. "Working" as a driver on the side from his legitimate business, he got more and more involved with Rocco's crew and started hanging out with the really hardcore wiseguys. One of those wiseguys was Johnny "The Hit." Guess where that nickname came from. And Johnny didn't like when people fucked with him. The following scene in one of the Bensonhurst bars, notoriously famous among the police for being a wiseguy hangout, proves it just about perfectly. Renzo still feels bad that he couldn't witness it himself, but the story quickly made its rounds among the crew the following day after it happened.

"Who the fuck does he think he is?! I'm not someone who you can disrespect like that and not pay for it!!!"

"Johnny, relax, you've been drinking, he's been drinking, let it slide! You won't even remember anything tomorrow!" Curly, another mad man from the "family," was trying to calm his enraged friend down; he knew that it wouldn't take long for Johnny "The Hit" to make big trouble. And big trouble meant a dead body and getting rid of that dead body, and that included special instruments, a lot of acid and a long trip to the Jersey Shore…

"Oh, I'm as sober as sober can be, my friend!" Johnny said. "I understand that he might straighten everything out with Rocco, but he still owes *me* the money! And he tells his friends that he'll pay me when *he* wants?! Are you fuckin kidding me?! That asshole forgot his place, that's what I tell you. And I'll show him where it is, it's six feet in the fuckin ground, that's where! And I'll drop dead right here if I don't put him there!!!"

The ongoing feud between Johnny and the guy he was actively cursing out, Junior, had been going on for years now. And the constant rivalry and a lot of bad blood between the two men had finally reached its climax, when an arrogant Junior had decided to flex his muscles and talk shit about Johnny in front of the others. That's when the long-lived animosity really had escalated and resulted in this conversation that Johnny was now having with his good buddy Curly.

"Johnny, he's just an idiot who can't tell his head from his ass, that's all! Yes, he disrespected you, but you don't really have to kill the guy! Just send the guys to beat him up a little, to teach him a lesson, but don't do anything stupid, I beg you! I'll run out of money for gas soon if we keep going to Jersey every fuckin week!"

"You're getting a soft spot, Curly. It's not good for business."

"I'm not getting a soft spot, I just..."

"He just reminds you of your older brother who passed away, God rest his soul. I know, we all know, but unlike your father, his father didn't teach that fucker good manners! And if I don't teach him now, soon every single roach will be spitting on us as if nothing happened. And I have a reputation to keep. If I don't teach this prick a lesson, Rocco's guys will teach me. It's an animal world, Curly. Kill or be killed. We can't show weakness. And in this case, forgiveness is a weakness."

Curly sighed and took a sip of his scotch. No matter how much he hated to admit it, Johnny was right. Even though Junior, who was stupid enough to cross one of the most merciless hitmen in Brooklyn, indeed reminded him much of his brother. But there was nothing he could do for the guy now. It's an animal world.

Then a couple of their friends walked into the bar. They shook hands with Johnny and Curly, kissing and hugging each other according to the old Italian tradition. They ordered their drinks (which, as Johnny immediately told the bartender, were on him) and started the regular mobster gossip: what does the boss say about this guy, who got in trouble this time, who forgot to pay on time and who didn't make it to the end of the week (because they forgot to pay on time, of course). And as soon as the door to the bar opened again, the list of people who didn't make it till the end of the week became one name longer.

Junior stepped inside, immediately turning all heads in his direction. The silence in the room became so obvious you could almost touch it. The bartender stopped cleaning his glasses and prepared to duck under the bar: he had worked in that bar long enough to know the drill. But Junior didn't plan on dying that day, so he slowly backed out of the door, without turning his back on the group at the bar. As soon as the door closed after him, the bartender sighed in relief, no shooting in his bar today! Johnny, however, got up from his chair and slowly walked to the entrance, every step of his shiny black shoes sounding like a nail in someone's coffin. After he made his exit, the crew returned to their drinks, obviously deciding to let the two straighten things out between them, even if for one of them it meant going home filled with bullets. They weren't involved in the conflict, and in their minds they silently agreed with Johnny: *you want to play gangster—one day you'll have to face a real one*.

Two muffled gunshots, as if someone opened two champagne bottles one right after another, could be heard right outside the bar; Johnny always used the silencer.

Curly walked to the window and pursed his lips. "He got him in his car."

The guys at the bar just nodded, and as soon as Johnny came back in, they got him a fresh drink. Then one of the guys followed with a smartass joke, "Why would you shoot the guy? He had really nice shoes on!"

Without saying a word, Johnny "The Hit" finished his drink in one shot, got up and went back outside. In less than a minute he came back with a pair of nice shiny wing tip shoes and put them on the bar right in front of his friend.

"You like them?" Johnny asked. "They're yours now. That fuckin asshole won't be needing them anymore."

"Don't put them on the bar! That's sick! They still have blood on them!"

"Too fuckin bad."

The men soon finished their drinks and took the two cars to go to dinner at one of the Italian restaurants in the area. The bartender took another deep sigh of relief, took his more than generous tip from the bar and continued business as usual. Before long New York's Finest showed up at the bar asking questions.

"I think I heard shots outside my bar…" the bartender told the cops. "I don't know, I've seen some Spanish guys hanging around outside. I'm pretty sure one of them might have had a gun."

Johnny and his crew were the kind of guys who would get up in the morning and as soon as their feet touched the floor, the devil would say, "Oh, shit! They're up!"

Renzo hoped to become one of them pretty soon.

Renzo, a “gangster-in-training,” finally decided to settle down. He was getting closer to his thirties and started thinking of having a family. His girlfriend of seven years had been bugging him about a proposal for quite some time, and Renzo finally decided to get her a ring. But even at that turning point in his life, he turned it into a joke: instead of bringing Lydia a small black box for Christmas as she was expecting and getting down on one knee as the tradition prescribes, he showed up at her door with a huge box, which had “stereo system” written on it.

“What the hell is that?” Lydia’s face said it all, and Renzo was kind of glad they weren’t in the kitchen with a bunch of knives for Lydia to use.

“What do you mean?” Renzo said. “That’s your Christmas present!”

“A stereo system?”

“Yeah! It’s awesome! Guys in the store said it had a really cool sound! Why don’t you go ahead and open it?”

“Why don’t I cut your neck open instead?” Lydia said, but nevertheless started to open the big box. To her surprise, it was full of books. “What is that, Renzo? Did you rob a library?”

“No, I put the books on top so I wouldn’t scratch it. Take them out.”

One by one Lydia started to take the books out of the box, until on the very bottom she found the little black box she had been waiting seven years for.

"Renzo, you're such an asshole! Even with this, you had to torture me?!"

"Well, if you want to get married, you have to suffer for it. After all, I'll be suffering my whole life!"

"Jerk!"

Renzo and Lydia were officially engaged.

Two Christmases later they were all celebrating the New Year in Renzo's Pool Room on the second floor of his sign shop. There was Renzo, his wife, Lydia, pregnant with their first child, some of their family members and a bunch of guys from Bensonhurst, including Johnny "The Hit," Curly, and Renzo's friends Sammy, Joey and Smiley. Everybody was having a good time; they were partying, playing pool, dancing and of course drinking a lot. However, one of the guys who had just started working for Renzo, named Marty, drank more than he should have and started getting more and more aggressive. For no particular reason, he also was getting louder and louder and was getting in the face of one of Renzo's buddies, Frankie. Renzo nicely offered him to take a walk and not ruin the party for the rest of the many guests that were there for this annual party.

"I don't give a fuck about your fuckin guests!" Marty yelled. "You think you're a tough guy, huh?"

Renzo just lifted both hands in the air, palms toward Marty's face, as a universal sign of peace, which was one of his signature moves, just like a rattle snake shakes its tale before it attacks. "Look, buddy, I don't want no trouble—"

Boom! Next thing you knew, Renzo had knocked the obnoxious idiot off his feet so fast that no one even noticed how it happened. "Now get the fuck out of my place and make sure I don't ever see you again! Or it's gonna be the last fuckin time you'll be seeing daylight!"

The guy slowly got up from the floor, staggering more from Renzo's punch than from being drunk, wiped the blood from his broken nose and fixed his eyes on Renzo. It looked like all the alcohol in him had evaporated, replaced by anger instead. After all, this guy was an Irish guy, and Irishmen don't like being punched in the face in front of everybody. All the guests were now watching them with interest, ready to jump in if Renzo needed them.

"You fucking asshole! You have no idea who you just hit! It's gonna be you who won't see the fucking daylight anymore, because I'll put you in the ground so deep that even the whole fucking K9 Unit of New York State won't be able to find you!"

"Oh yeah?" Renzo was seeing red as well but gave the man one more chance to get away before giving him a major ass-kicking. "Make sure you don't throw up all over yourself trying, you seem to be very close to it now!"

"I'll cut you up into little pieces. I'll cut up your wife and your unborn baby into little pieces, and all your family members, just to make sure that none of you walk this Earth anymore."

With these words the guy reached in his sport coat's inside pocket and produced a knife, holding it with all the determination of an angry man who had decided to "protect his dignity," even though he was the one who had started the whole thing. That last gesture triggered not only Renzo, but Johnny "The Hit," who was watching the young man closely to later report to Rocco about how his protégé handled a potentially dangerous situation. Johnny didn't like nasty drunks who would start threatening their host with a knife in the middle of a party they were lucky to get invited to; more than that, he didn't like when they would fall as low as threatening somebody's wife, which was one of the biggest taboos in the world of the Italian mafia. Men killed men; touching a woman was off limits. Ready to jump on this guy at any second, he nevertheless decided to give Renzo a chance to show what he was capable of, and the pissed off Renzo was capable of a lot of scary things.

First things first, Renzo quickly disarmed Marty—Mike's workouts clearly had a lot to do with his fast-as-lightning skills—and threw his knife behind the bar, where he wouldn't be able to get to it any time soon. Then he started punching him, quickly taking over him, even though this guy was really tough. After punching the shit out of the guy, Renzo took him by the collar of his jacket and threw him down the stairs.

“Be so kind as to show yourself out! I’m busy with my ‘fucking guests!’”

With those words Renzo returned to the room, accompanied by the cheers and whistles of the guys, patting him on the back and handing him a drink right away. Renzo wiped his bloody hands on a towel and was ready to get back to partying, but this guy wasn’t the kind who gave up so quickly. He had somehow managed to climb the stairs and was just about to jump on Renzo’s back, when Frankie intercepted him mid-move, grabbing him by the neck and hitting him in the head with his massive fist about ten times in a row. Renzo didn’t want to miss out on the action, and after Frankie was done he gladly added a couple of kicks to the guy’s ribs. After throwing the guy down the stairs for a second time, the men followed his crippled body this time, making sure the asshole wouldn’t be making any comebacks any time soon. Each of Marty’s efforts to kick back at his opponents was met with a shower of new punches, which put him into a blissful half-comatose state. After making sure that the stubborn prick was unconscious and wasn’t a threat to anybody in the house, the two started to discuss what to do with him next.

“We can’t just leave him here,” Renzo said, “he’s gonna bleed all over my carpet, this fuckin asshole! Let’s get him out!”

"Out where?" Frankie said. "You want to just dump him outside like some bum? The police will be here in five seconds!"

"They wouldn't even know it's a human body! Look at him, he looks like a fuckin pile of rags, ha ha! But seriously, let's just get him home somehow."

"Yeah, that's probably a good idea. Let his poor wife deal with this motherfucker!"

"He ain't got no wife, Frankie! She ran away with the fuckin baker from across the street!"

"I wonder why!"

Meanwhile Johnny came walking into the room with a big hunting knife and a plastic garbage bag. "Let's cut him up and put the pieces in this garbage bag and then throw it in your dumpster!"

"Jesus, Johnny!" Renzo said. "Is that your answer to everything?! The guy works here! They'll trace it back to me in a minute, and his fucking DNA is all over the place!"

Renzo's brain was racing now, *What to do, what to do? I got it!* He ran outside to flag down a cab. He got lucky in just a couple of minutes, when a yellow cab pulled over next to his shop.

"My friend," Renzo said, "I have a drunk buddy of mine, who's in desperate need of a ride home. And don't worry, he won't throw up, he's not in any condition to."

"No problem, boss, get him in."

Renzo returned to the shop and helped Frankie get the heavy as a dead man inside the car.

"His address is on his driver license right here," Renzo told the cabbie. "Here's two hundred bucks, get him home."

"Wait, wait, whoa, whoa, whoa! He's all covered in blood! Is he still alive? You can't leave him in my car! What did you guys do to him?"

"He's fine, trust me, just get him home, and he'll be like a new guy tomorrow."

"I'm not gonna take this guy, he'll bleed all over my car!"

Renzo took a gun out of his jacket and pushed it into the driver's temple. "I said, here's two hundred dollars. Take this fuckin guy home or you're both gonna look like twins. Do we have a problem here?"

"No, boss, no problem at all! I'm sorry… just please let me go, I'll be on my way and won't say a word about what I saw here! No problem at all, boss!"

"Didn't think so. Remember, I see your name on your taxi license, and I know where you live!"

The driver, happy to get away alive, took off like a bandit, and Renzo just exchanged a look with Frankie and laughed.

"You're a crazy guy," Frankie said, "you know?"

"Yeah… I've been told that a couple of times."

"Let's go back inside. I think we had some serious drinking to do before we were so rudely interrupted. And Johnny is waiting for us, and we don't want to disappoint him!"

Chapter 6

"Boys and Their Toys"

"There's nothing—absolutely nothing—half so much worth doing as messing about in boats."

(K. Grahame)

Renzo always liked extreme situations, let it be car chases, fights, drugs or shootings. So when he got an opportunity to add some more extreme to his life by getting a boat from his father's friend, he wasn't going to miss it for anything. Of course it was a powerboat; Renzo would never get a sailboat just because it would be so slow that it would annoy the shit out of him, number one, and number two, it would get in the way of all the "normal" boats that are always racing near the marina. As a getaway driver for Rocco and his guys, Renzo had already mastered his driving skills next to perfection, so he needed something new to get his adrenaline rush from. And the powerboat seemed like an ideal solution.

It was a beautiful, almost new 27 ft. boat with the nicest wooden deck, a kitchen and a bar downstairs. It became Renzo's favorite toy for about a year, till he mastered his boating skills and decided to go for a bigger boat, a 37 ft. model. Since Renzo was a perfectionist—whatever he would start doing in life, he wanted to become the best at it, let it be the toughest fighter, the fastest driver or the funniest guy in the club—he decided to take his new hobby very seriously and applied for boating classes at St. Francis College in Brooklyn. He wanted to know everything that could help him to become one of the best boaters at the marina; another reason was that he had heard too many stories about the unpredictable coastal weather and how too many inexperienced sailors almost or actually died because they were careless or stupid enough to think that they could outsmart the fierce Atlantic storms, suddenly catching them in open waters. But Renzo somehow turned even such a serious matter as college boating classes into his own private comedy club.

Originally it was four of them: Renzo and his friends Georgie, Barry and Smitty; the speed freaks, who pretty soon became known as the Sea-Rays, taken from the name of the manufacturer that was producing the fastest luxury powerboats at that time. And it should be noted that it just so happens that in every boating school there's an ongoing feud between the powerboaters and the sailboaters, who are always made fun of by the speed freaks.

We had this initiation process as soon as the teacher would introduce a new student to the class. We were kind of the badass guys, always sitting in the back of the class and making funny comments, you know, just like in high school. And the new student was supposed to say a few words about himself, just to introduce himself, and after that the teacher would normally ask them what kind of boat he had. So if the guy said he had a speed boat, we started cheering and whistling, screaming "yeah, a powerboat!" and applauding the guy. But God forbid the newbie said he had a sailboat; then we booed to no end and did just about everything but tear him a second asshole! Even the teacher couldn't calm us down. We were the wiseguys of the class.

We had this teacher, Mr. Adams, he was very cool. And you wouldn't believe it, but he had a sailboat. Well, actually, when he was younger, he was a devoted powerboater, but as he got older he got himself something calmer. So we didn't really goof on him for that, we only said that "once you're a powerboater, you'll always be a powerboater, and no girly sailboat will ever change it." He laughed.

Mr. Adams taught us a lot of things, like how to somewhat predict the weather by the pressure outside, how to find out how far away a storm was, how to drive properly during a storm so the waves wouldn't sink your boat; very useful stuff that I later used in my boating practice and which made me very grateful to Mr. Adams for all of his lessons. A couple of those lessons even saved my life once or twice.

After four years in college and almost completing the courses for his captain's license, Renzo was feeling confident enough in his boating skills to start doing all the crazy stuff that Renzo wouldn't have been Renzo without. He really tried to observe the rules, but when he was born, God had decided that Renzo would be the guy who would always break all of them. A decision that affected Renzo's whole life, but even God needs someone to entertain Him.

Famous among the boaters was this Jersey hotel named Molly Pitcher, and Renzo and his family and friends would often go there to enjoy both the marina and the outside bar. However, some of Renzo's friends sometimes enjoyed the bar a little too much, and the results were quite unpredictable and sometimes life-threatening. Not for them though, but for the people around them, which was probably the most ironic part.

One beautiful June day, while his parents were enjoying the sun outside, Renzo and his buddies Georgie and Barry decided to hit the bar. Georgie, who was almost as crazy as Renzo, thought it would be a good idea to celebrate their recent graduation with a couple (or several couples) of scotches before they "hit the ocean." After some serious drinking was done, the buddies were all fired up for the boating adventure and left the small private harbor of Molly Pitcher each in his own boat.

Renzo didn't drink too much that day mainly for two reasons: first, he was still completing courses at the boating school to get a captain's license and didn't want to get in trouble with the harbor patrol if stopped for whatever reason; the second, and more important reason, was that he didn't want to get his ass kicked by his father, who had come out into the ocean with him and wouldn't appreciate the captain of his new boat being drunk. Georgie was by himself and already had his license, which, along with his long-time boating experience, made him feel confident enough to do the stupidest stuff an extreme boat-loving person on a powerboat was capable of. All those factors, combined with a couple of hours of boating, resulted in the following, very unfortunate incident.

The Molly Pitcher Hotel harbor was very small and narrow, with no wake buoys at the entrance to prevent boaters from going too fast and creating waves within the harbor, which could easily damage other people's boats tied up to the docks. All the normal people of course knew and understood the purpose of those buoys and would put their boats in a slow-go position before entering the harbor. But Georgie, fueled by some hardcore scotch and his own ego, decided to show his friends, who were following behind his boat in a line, "how the big boys park their boats" and entered the narrow harbor almost at full speed.

"Renzo, don't do anything stupid," Frank said from beside him. He knew his son's competitive side too well and decided to prevent any "harbor racing" even before such an idea could visit his son's mind. "Let that idiot do whatever he wants, you go slow. The management here is very tough, and they will not only ban us from staying at their hotel for life but will also report you to the coastguard. And those are more problems than you need."

"I'm not doing anything, Dad."

"I know what you're thinking though."

Renzo just shook his head and slowly proceeded into the harbor. Meanwhile, one of the harbor supervisors, absolutely enraged by Georgie's speeding, started yelling at him from the shore to stop his boat immediately, but Georgie at that point was having too much fun to follow the "supervisor's nerdy orders." Pissed off to no end by such disobedience, the guy jumped right into his own boat, and being in a rush to catch Georgie, did a very stupid thing he regretted just seconds later.

Now if you don't know the principle of starting a boat, the very first rule is that before you start the engines, you MUST release all the gas fumes from the bilge, which is where the motor is positioned, by turning on the blowers for five minutes, otherwise a spark from the engines could easily cause a Hiroshima explosion. But the harbor supervisor was so caught up in his emotions that he completely forgot about this very important rule, and what Renzo saw several moments later was a huge ball of fire that made the supervisor's boat almost jump out of the water and land back into it in pieces. The supervisor, who luckily only suffered some second degree burns as it turned out later, landed in the water near his burning boat, screaming for help.

Despite his mother's screams that he's going to get himself and them all killed, Renzo drove as close as he could to the still burning boat to pick up the lucky survivor. The guy was burned, but not too badly; he was mostly just suffering from the shock. He was wrapped in a blanket right away and delivered by Renzo to the shore, where the hotel medical staff picked him up. Renzo later told the story to all his friends and family, making fun of his mom and saying that while the poor guy was trying to grab the boat's side, she was taking his fingers off it one-by-one, saying, "Every man for himself! Get off our boat!!!"

The poor woman got all embarrassed and kept saying, "Renzo, stop! I didn't do or say any of it!"

Meanwhile Georgie, pretty shaken up by the story, which he was the cause of, took off from the scene like a bandit. When asked about the guy who was the reason that the supervisor's boat blew up, Renzo just shrugged and answered that he's pretty sure the guy was just some nut whom he never saw in his life. If you came from Bensonhurst, you didn't rat your friends out, no matter what stupid shit they did.

However, the "don't rat on your friends" rule didn't mean that you couldn't prank their ass as a form of payback for all the stress they had caused you, at least according to Renzo's thinking. When the burnt supervisor called him up several days later to thank him again for saving his life by risking his own, Renzo was very glad to hear that he was doing OK and said that he wished he knew who the guy behind the whole accident was, so he could kick his ass personally. In a couple of weeks, to Renzo's big surprise, he received a summons, ordering him to appear in court because of the accident. As it turned out, there was a mix-up, and the coast guard accidentally assumed it was Renzo's fault because his boat was the one they had seen closest to the scene of the accident. But the supervisor straightened it all right out, making sure that Renzo received nothing but his gratitude.

The whole summons thing though gave Renzo the perfect setup to get his payback on Georgie. The following day, when Renzo saw Georgie, he showed him the summons and said that he had no other option but to tell the judge the truth, otherwise he'd be the one to go to jail. Georgie's face went white, and he started begging his friend not to rat him out.

“Man, I can’t cover your ass here,” Renzo told him. “I’m not going to jail because you did some stupid thing, I just can’t…” He played his part so naturally that he turned poor Georgie into a paranoiac for a good couple of days.

After a couple of hundred phone calls of begging and offerings from Georgie, Renzo finally cracked up and told the poor guy that he was only messing with him. Georgie had never been so happy in his life.

Renzo loved messing with his friends, and his Oscar-worthy acting never left any room for doubts. Everybody believed him: cops, mobsters, his friends—not a single person was immune to Renzo’s mind games. He still refers to himself as a “professional bullshitter,” and frankly speaking if he were to just stop working this instant and start a career as a public speaker, teaching salesmen, politicians and lawyers how to professionally bullshit people, he would become a millionaire in just a couple of months. But he’s having too much fun being a Brooklyn boy to make such a drastic career change, and it wouldn’t work too well anyway because he would probably give somebody a beating for asking him a stupid question after his lecture. So he just entertains himself at the expense of others and lets other people learn his tricks by watching him for free.

The boat somehow became yet just another setting for Renzo's tricks, and quite a few of his friends were at some point affected by it. One time, not too long after Renzo got his first boat, he decided to give his business partner Richard a ride, since it was a weekend and a nice warm summer day. They were almost under the Verrazano Bridge, when it suddenly started to drizzle. Since Renzo was the only one of the two of them who could drive the boat, he asked Rich to go to the front and snap down the cover so they wouldn't get soaking wet; the rain seemed to be getting stronger and stronger. Suspecting nothing from his good friend Renzo, who completely stopped the boat to give his buddy a chance to snap on the cover, Richard was balancing on the polished fiberglass bow holding only onto the windshield, when Renzo suddenly gave the boat the full throttle.

Richard started screaming at Renzo that he was trying to kill him, but Renzo was just laughing his ass off going faster and faster. Trying to get a better grip and not slide off the slippery boat nose, Rich grabbed a windshield wiper, but Renzo, who seemed to be enjoying every second of his friend's misery, turned them on.

"What the fuck are you doing, you asshole???" Rich yelled. "I'm going to fall off!"

Renzo, still laughing, pretended that he couldn't hear him, "What are you saying? The wind is too strong when you're going this fast, I can't hear you!"

"So stop fucking going full speed!!!"

"What? You want me to go full speed? OK!"

Finally after a minute of living hell for Richard, Renzo finally stopped the boat and helped his friend get back inside, but only after he took a nice picture of him almost hanging off the side of the boat. They both still keep it, one as proof of his strong grip, another as proof of his sick sense of humor, but both always laugh pretty hard when they remember the story.

Richard was the first, but actually not the only guy to ride the nose of the boat while Renzo was giving it the full throttle. Renzo played the same trick with several more friends, and when he got a bigger boat, which pretty soon got the name of "the party boat" because of all the parties Renzo was throwing almost every weekend, he started doing it as a special trick to entertain his guests.

Renzo's parties were probably the craziest boat parties you can possibly imagine: they always included a bunch of crazy Italian guys (and sometimes Russian ones too, as by that time some of them were working for Renzo and were always up for a good party), hot girls in bikinis or cocktail dresses, the loudest stereo system around and lots and lots and lots, and I really mean lots, of liquor. Maybe just a little bit of drugs too. In other words, Renzo's boat was nothing less than a floating Studio 54. And just like Steve Rubell, crazy Renzo was always making sure his guests were having the best time of their lives. Many times, after loading the boat with food and alcohol they would cruise at night—when normal people would never take their boats out since you can't see shit in the open ocean in the middle of the night—and they partied like there was no tomorrow.

One time, before it got too dark, they saw another boat not too far from their marina entrance and drove a little closer to say hello. The boat belonged to a German man who charted tours coming up from Florida. He had a 60' sailboat booked full of Germans who barely spoke any English and was taking them all the way up the coast to Maine. Once in the marina, the German captain gave Renzo a tour of the beautiful boat, and all the electronics and equipment that were on board simply fascinated Renzo. They had machines that printed out weather reports and every possible accommodation you could imagine to comfortably hold fifteen men on board. Renzo, ever the smart ass, told them, "You have every possible accommodation on this boat… but where do you keep the women?"

Their faces went from shock to outright belly-shaking laughter. They immediately loved Renzo's wit and personality.

Judging by the fact that all of them were almost sober and just resting in the marina, Renzo shook his head and said that the German guy's boat party must have sucked and if they wanted to be at a real American party, they better jump onto his boat before it got too late. The poor Germans never drank so much in their entire lives as when they drank on Renzo's boat. Their generous host even offered them a nice sightseeing tour around the City at full speed. After that he took them to the

Statue of Liberty, and drove the boat so close to it that the Statue almost picked up her leg and said, "What the hell do you think you're doing, man? Come on, stop messing around, you're getting my skirt wet!"

Taking into consideration the amount of alcohol they drank that night, there was a very strong possibility that some of them really saw the Statue talk. The Germans were delivered to the shore safe but not so sound. The very next morning they left a bottle of scotch on Renzo's boat and a note reading, "We had the time of our lives! Thank you for your hospitality, and we hope to see you again next year on our yearly trip up the coast!" It was signed, "The Germans."

Renzo just laughed and said, "Hey guys! We're all American ambassadors now!"

Having a boat could get them not only to the sites, but also to the hottest near-water City spots. One time when Renzo was throwing yet another famous party on his boat with a bunch of model-looking girls on board, he and Vito decided to take all their guests for a nice dinner at a popular restaurant by the Chelsea Piers. The maître d', however, wasn't so enthusiastic about accommodating about thirty people with no reservation at a half hour notice, and after snobbishly saying that the restaurant had no available tables, he hung up on them. Since Renzo never took "no" for an answer, he just shrugged and kept driving to the Chelsea Piers. But prior to pulling up to the entrance, he lined up all the hot, tiny bikini-clad ladies on board right where everyone could see them… on the bow! Every male patron's jaw dropped at that point, and the dock boys were all frantically fighting to tie up the boat and escort the girls off to the best table in the house.

Renzo stood there nodding his head. "It's always all about the girls, Vito, isn't it?"

Vito just smirked and answered, "Yup!"

Another one of Renzo's favorite tricks was to let his friends hold the wheel at the most unsuitable times and scare the shit out of them to the point where they almost believed they were going to die any minute. One of the first of Renzo's unfortunate buddies to experience this was Mikey, and Mikey loved taking little trips with Renzo in his new, big boat, especially up the Hudson River. One of the great things about the Hudson River is that if you go all the way up, you can actually reach Canada (Mikey knew about that), but another interesting fact about the Hudson River is that from time to time huge barges follow the same route as the powerboats and the sailboats, creating a lot of problems for the latter (Mikey didn't know about that, and Renzo immediately used it to his advantage of course).

Seeing a big barge coming toward them and knowing the nature of the water in the very narrow River, Renzo acted out the following scenario like a first class actor: he kindly asked Mikey to hold the wheel while he would go downstairs to "use the bathroom." Mikey was more than happy to complete the task, hoping to later brag to his friends that he drove a boat all by himself. Little did he know that his good friend Renzo meanwhile was holding on for his life downstairs, preparing for the first huge wave. A few seconds later, the wave made the boat jump out of the water and almost took poor Mikey off his feet. Renzo knew that the second wake would be even bigger, and as it came seconds after, he couldn't help but laugh when he heard Mikey screaming upstairs, "Renzo!!! Something's wrong!!! Come get the wheel nooooow!!!"

The third wave, which was also the biggest one, made the boat airborne and freaked Mikey out to the point where he just held on for his life and screamed at the top of his lungs, "Reeeeenzoooooo!!!!!"

After just a few more smaller waves passed and the water became nice and still again, Renzo finally came out from his little "shelter" and gave Mikey his best surprised look.

"Mikey? What the hell did you do to the boat? I almost broke my face off on the bathroom sink! Who the fuck drives like that?! You almost got us both killed!"

Mikey, white as a ghost but obviously happy that he was still alive and breathing, apologized to his friend as if it really was his fault, "Man, I'm so sorry! I have no idea what the fuck happened! I thought we were going to frigging die!"

"Well, I thought I was going to die in the frigging toilet! Do you know how embarrassing that would have been?"

After a long pause Mikey finally realized that Renzo was just messing with him and play-punched him in the shoulder. "You're such an asshole, man! You knew it would happen, didn't you? You just went and set me up, you fuck!"

"I couldn't help it. You should have seen your face, man! And the way you screamed like a little girl was just priceless! Totally worth it!"

All joking aside, several times the storms were not made up by Renzo to mess with his friends but were very real and very life-threatening. The scariest kind of the Atlantic storms are the summer squalls, which are absolutely unpredictable and come as fast as they go, sometimes lasting as little as fifteen minutes but leaving behind devastation and sinking boats as if they were a full force hurricane. The radar doesn't detect them, and they say that if you see them, it's already too late. So after you spot a quickly approaching black wall of clouds, you basically have two choices: try to outrun it (but only if you're close to your home base or a nearby marina) or drive right through it.

One time Renzo and his father, Frank, were lucky enough to make it safely back to the marina and tie the boat up right before the storm hit the shore. As soon as they had first noticed that something funny was coming on the horizon, Renzo turned his boat around to the shore and gave it full speed.

"Renzo, you're never gonna make it back!" Frank had a tendency to be negative pretty much about everything, especially at times like this, which didn't help his son a tiny bit, but annoyed the crap out of him instead.

"Dad, you're not helping me being a negative Nancy, so please just don't say nothing and let me concentrate on driving!"

After about ten minutes of racing with the insanely fast approaching storm, they finally made it safely to the marina just in time to tie up the boat as tightly as they could and find shelter down below. For a good twenty minutes they were holding on for their lives as the boat rocked around like a roller coaster. And all that time Renzo kept laughing and telling his dad, "What did I tell you? I told you we would make it!"

Frank kept his face straight as if it didn't really impress him, but deep down he was proud of his crazy son.

But not all boaters were as lucky as Renzo, and this one time Renzo's "boat neighbor" and retired detective Matt experienced the full immense force of a fast-moving Atlantic storm, which caught him and his boating buddy Tom just outside the marina. The weather that day had been absolutely beautiful, and there hadn't been a sign of the approaching storm in the sky. Matt and Tom left the marina and headed to the ocean in Matt's fishing boat to enjoy the cool ocean breeze on a hot summer day; a little behind them there was another boat following their route, it belonged to another guy from the marina, Randy. Before separating, they waved to each other and wished each other a great day on the radio. No one could have expected what was about to happen just moments later.

Matt was the first one to see that something weird was going on. His fishing boat was designed in a way that the captain was supposed to sail it from the very top, known as a Tuna Tower, and the top was a good 15-20 ft. higher than all other regular boats.

"Hey, Tom! I think there's a storm coming our way! It doesn't look too pretty, the sky is all black!"

Tom, who was doing something on the first level, quickly climbed the stairs to the top, where Matt was sitting, and now was able to see quite a frightening picture himself.

"Holy shit!!! It's coming right our way!" Tom said. "Shall we turn back while we're not too far from the marina yet?"

"I don't think it's a good idea, buddy. The boat is not the fastest, and if this thing catches us from behind, that's it, we're going to sink."

"So what do you propose we do?"

"Nothing, we stay right where we are and keep the boat facing right into it."

It was obvious that Tom was more than skeptical about the whole "driving right through it" idea and would have much rather preferred if his captain had changed his mind and turned back before it got too late. After all, they were just right outside the marina, how long would it take them to get back?

"Do you think it's a good idea?" Tom asked. "All those black clouds don't look too good to me."

"Well, we don't have too much of a choice at this point. The only chance to survive this storm is to face it."

Tom just sighed and decided to rely on his friend, who had more than twenty years of boating experience under his belt and so probably knew what he was doing. At least Tom prayed to God that he did. Randy, however, another boater who had also spotted the storm, which was now coming their way so fast that it was impossible to miss it, made up his mind in a split second and quickly started to turn his boat around to go back.

"Oh, look, Randy is turning back!" Tom thought that maybe this argument would make Matt change his mind and follow the other boat back home.

"That's not a good idea," Matt said. "I really hope he makes it back, but he should have just stayed right where he was!"

After just a couple of minutes, when the first big wave hit the boat, Tom wasn't so sure that Matt had made the right decision.

"Whatever you do now, Tom, just hold on to these metal railings! No matter what, don't let go!!!"

The only way you can ride through a storm like that is to keep the nose pointed right at the waves. During those mini-hurricanes the gusts of wind get so strong that if you don't manage to keep your boat straight, it only takes two or three big waves to fill one side of your boat with water and sink it within seconds. The even worse case scenario is if the storm catches you from behind, while you're trying to escape it. Then you multiply your chances to catch one good wave right over the back of your boat, which is always lower than the front, and that'll be more than enough to sink it right away. That's exactly what happened to Randy: a huge wave got his brand new 47' Viking sport fishing boat right at the entrance of the marina, and within a minute the only thing that was left of it were two antennas sticking out of the water. Luckily for Randy, he was right next to the big rocks at the entrance of the marina, from where the locals later saved him. The boat, however, was just gone.

Tom, who saw all that happen, now knew for sure that his buddy Matt had made the right decision, but this realization didn't make the whole situation easier. The wind was so strong that it completely ripped off the cover from the top of the boat, and now the two men were literally face-to-face with the vicious storm. To make things worse, huge pieces of ice the size of golf balls started coming down, pelting the poor men's faces and bodies. The boat was rocking so hard that at some point they got so close to the water that they probably could have touched it with their hands even though they were at the very top of the boat.

The storm passed as quickly as it had come, and Matt actually saw it pass them like a wall and go farther out to sea. In front of them were clear blue skies and calm waters; the two friends, however, looked like they had been jumped by twenty guys, that's how badly their faces had been beaten and bruised by the ice. Right after that storm Matt was ready to sell his boat and never go back to the ocean again, but just like a cowboy who always gets back on his horse even after a bad fall, he was back to the marina right after his injuries healed.

When Renzo saw him the day after the storm, he couldn't believe what had happened to his buddy and just kept telling him how lucky he was to be alive. To this day when Renzo and Matt get together at the marina, Renzo tells everybody about his crazy buddy Matt who rode out that storm and "kicked its ass."

One time Renzo also had an incident that almost sank his boat, but unlike all the normal people who have this problem because of normal reasons like storms, Renzo caused it himself during one of his Studio 54-like parties in the middle of the night. This time it was a boys night out, and in particular they were celebrating Renzo's Russian partner's friend on the boat. The guy's name was Alex, and he was afraid of pretty much any kind of water that wasn't bottled in his fridge or running in his shower. Renzo and his partner Edward finally talked him into taking a nice ride with them on a beautiful powerboat, on a warm and breezy August night. What could possibly go wrong? Well, nothing really, except for Renzo's stunt driving after approximately a gallon of scotch and God knows what else.

The reason why normal people don't sail at night is because the visibility is zero and you can't even see your own hand, let alone other boats or objects in the water. And that's exactly how Renzo hit the telephone pole, which made a pretty big impact, breaking his stuffing box, which houses the propeller shaft and keeps the water from coming into the bilge where the engines are. While Renzo was partying in the front of the boat, Edward noticed that something funny was happening at the back.

"Hey, bud, I think we have some kind of a problem. There's steam coming from down below."

Renzo at first thought that his partner was just bullshitting him, but as soon as he went to check what was going on and opened the floor panels to the bilge compartment, he sobered up right away. "Oh, shit!"

Having been a knowledgeable boater for quite some time, Renzo knew that losing one engine wasn't good at all and that they would be lucky to make it back to shore. So, first thing, he immediately turned the boat around and started calling the coast guard on the radio.

"Mayday, Mayday! We've got a big problem here!"

Meanwhile Alex, who quickly realized that something wasn't right, anxiously started yanking on Renzo's shirt. "Renzo? What's going on? Doesn't 'Mayday' mean we're sinking?"

"Well… actually yes, that's exactly what it means, Al!" Even in situations such as this, Renzo was still breaking people's balls. And seeing Alex's face turn white as a ghost cracked him up. "Don't worry, we're not too far from the shore, and they're coming to get us!"

"What???"

Let me just note that Alex had been bragging about his new shoes prior to getting on the boat and Renzo had admired them. So with all this going on Renzo told him, "At this point in time, if I were you, I would take off those nice new shoes and put them somewhere higher up in the boat so they won't get wet."

Alex's face became very long, in addition to being pale.

"Renzo… I think I'm gonna die of a heart attack. Please tell me this isn't true!"

"I wish I could my buddy… I've been boating for almost ten years, and I ain't never seen a situation as bad as this… Now where's my scotch?"

Renzo quickly fetched the life jackets (and scotch) from downstairs and started handing them out to all his passengers, which freaked out the poor Russian guy even more.

"Renzo please!!! What's up with the jackets?"

"Just put it on, it's the law."

"Why do I need a jacket, Renzo? Are we really sinking???"

"Well, if you're a good swimmer, you don't need a jacket."

"Renzo, I can't swim at all!!! I hate water!!!"

"Well, in this case I would strongly recommend you put it on."

With one engine partially underwater, the second one was working twice as hard, trying to get them back to the marina as fast as the boat could go even as more water continued gushing in. Renzo knew that they only had minutes till the water killed another engine, and then he would lose the boat for sure. The coast guards' boat caught them almost at the entrance of the marina and escorted them inside, where other boaters were already waiting with the big power water pumps. By then the back of Renzo's boat was already underwater.

Finally they reached the shore, and the other boaters in the marina with their electric and hand pumps jumped into action right away. But the boat already had so much water in it that they quickly realized that all of their efforts would only be a waste of time. They needed something better than trying to pump the water out of the quickly sinking boat. Luckily for Renzo, one of the guys at the marina knew the marina crane operator, who was able to drive down within minutes and pick the boat up out of the water—the only solution they had at this point. Everybody was shocked to see how much water came out of the boat while it was hanging in the air, and the crane was hardly keeping up with holding its weight.

And one more time, Renzo cheated the devil. The poor Russian guy never came close to the ocean ever again and was now suspicious of his shower water as well. After an insane night that the whole marina was talking about for the next few months and about $20,000 cost in repairs for the boat, Renzo was ready to open his house party boat once again.

"This guy will never learn his lesson," his father, Frank, said and just shook his head.

"Well, we had fun though, didn't we?" Renzo replied and smiled at him.

His dad said through gritted teeth, "You'll never follow the rules, Renzo, will you?"

Chapter 7

"Grossberger and the Bike"

"Faster, faster, faster, until the thrill of speed overcomes the fear of death."

(H. Thompson)

Pretty soon boats weren't extreme enough for Renzo anymore, even with all the almost sinking, partying, escaping of storms and the pranking of friends. His marriage wasn't working out too well and was nothing like he had expected it to be, and now he found himself desperately looking for new ways to bring excitement into his life. He was now a father of two beautiful babies, but that was pretty much all the joy that had come out of his married life. In his late thirties, Renzo was still too young to let depression and disappointment get the best of him as it had gotten the best of some of his childhood friends. Instead of being miserable and silently suffering alone, drowning his sorrows in a glass of scotch, he decided to find something that would make his blood rush as if he was again a seventeen-year-old boy stealing cars just for the fun of it. That something was a brand new bike, which soon became his best friend and his partner in crime.

Renzo wasn't the only guy who preferred the chances of killing himself in a drunk driving accident to the chances of overdosing on drugs, which had already happened to some of his buddies. Here's how he found himself in a circle of bikers/wiseguys, that happened to be the craziest of both breeds and included his long-time Jewish friend, Ben (the same Ben who shot his girlfriend in the pussy when he found her in bed with some other guy), his father's friend who now had become his best friend, Vito (the same Vito who let Renzo and Ben in his top-notch night club right after Ben had gotten out of prison for shooting his girlfriend and her boyfriend), and some other nutty Bensonhurst guys, now all respectable gentlemen, who used to be the biggest troublemakers growing up with Renzo. But the new friend that Renzo made thanks to his new bike addiction could have easily outdone all the most insane neighborhood guys put together. His name was Grossberger.

Grossberger was a massive, over 300-pound killing machine. Just by walking into a store to buy some cigarettes at three in the morning, the cashier would offer him their cash register money, saying, "Here, take it all, I don't want any trouble!" Quite naturally, when Renzo, who was waiting for his biker friends in some diner in Staten Island, spotted Grossberger, who was also sitting by himself waiting for his biker friends, he immediately felt the urge to make friends with him.

Grossberger was, frankly speaking, quite surprised that someone wanted to start a conversation with him in the first place, and especially that the guy was a biker himself. At first he was a little standoffish, but after they talked across the room from separate tables for a few moments, Grossberger couldn't help but accept the brave stranger's offer to sit together while they both waited for their buddies to show up.

Fifteen minutes and a couple of drinks later, they were talking so enthusiastically about their bikes, and common friends who they knew and people they were associated with, that when Grossberger's friends finally showed up at the diner, they mistakenly thought that the two had known each other for many, many years. Grossberger and his buddies invited Renzo and his friends to ride together that day. It became the start of Renzo and Grossberger riding religiously together, as well as the starting point for a new era: the Bike Era, also known as the "drunk-riding-through-the-alligators-and-fighting-people-on-the-way" era. If Renzo was looking for excitement in his life, he had come to the right place!

Their private wiseguys/bikers club started with only three or four people riding only on Mondays, which very soon expanded to twenty and sometimes even thirty guys, gathering near Fort Hamilton on Shore Road in Brooklyn and loudly making their way to their usual hangout in the City, called "Hogs and Heifers." It was the sickest biker place you could possibly visit in Manhattan, with hot, Texas-style dressed bartenders setting the bar on fire and dancing on it, occasionally spitting fire out of their mouths all the way up to the black ceiling; with a wall fully decorated with bras, generously donated by the female patrons of the bar (Madonna's bra is still over there, and you can still touch it and even take a picture with it); and of course with its main attraction—New York City bikers, all out of their mind. That was the kind of setting in which Renzo and his friends fit just perfectly.

Alcohol flowed like a river, and every Monday night these guys partied harder than the rest of the Manhattan population did on Fridays. Some of them left the City barely able to walk, let alone ride a bike, and sometimes minor accidents happened. An example of one of those minor accidents was Willy's tunnel riding incident, which still causes a burst of laughter every time Renzo brings it up to his friends.

Willy has always been a fast rider, that nut! We would always street race, but at times when even I was smart enough to realize that it was too dangerous to ride so fast, he would still pass me by and squeeze all the power he could out of his poor bike! And especially if he was drinking—woo, forget about it! Just like this one time when we were coming back from the bar and had just entered the tunnel. That nut just had to accelerate so hard that he almost flew past us, but what he didn't think of was that he had to make a turn soon—and you know how it is in a tunnel, when you turn you can't really see where you're going until you come out of the turn. So after we made the turn, what did we see in front of us: two slow ass drivers going side-by-side at about 20 mph and our idiot, Willy, blowing by us at close to 100 mph. The only option he had to avoid crashing into the back of the car in the right lane was to squeeze himself between the car and the wall, which was exactly what he did… at 100 mph!!!

You should have seen the face of the poor car driver! He looked like he was having a heart attack. I bet he'd never seen a bike so close up, especially between him and a wall, both which made sparks shoot up as they rubbed against the bike's pipes and side bars… it was like the fucking Fourth of July! And what do you think Willy did? He pressed the accelerator even harder, jumped in front of the car and was gone!

We finally caught up with him after the tollbooth plaza: he was standing on the side of the road trying to fix his bike, which was all mangled up after what he had done to it in the tunnel! The handlebars were so bent that he couldn't even drive it properly, but we had Grossberger straighten them out (of course he did it with his bare hands!). We were lucky that Grossberger was with us that day, otherwise Willy would have been fucked. The driver of the car he had scratched pretty damn well was already talking to the tollbooth attendant and pointing at us, so we had to get out of there as soon as we could. We knew we had to separate, so we told Willy to go under the highway and we followed our usual route like nothing had happened on the upper highway. Two minutes later, three police cars caught up to us and pulled us over.

“What’s the problem, officer?” Of course I was the front man who did all the talking.

“You know pretty damn well what the problem is. Which one of you had an accident in the tunnel?” The cop wasn’t buying my innocent face, so I had to bullshit him some more.

“What accident?” I asked. “I have no idea what you’re talking about, officer. We didn’t have any accidents.”

“I’m not saying it was you. Maybe a buddy of yours who was riding with you, guys, and I need to know where he is.”

“None of us had any accidents, sir. Just take a look at our bikes, check them for any scratches, you’ll see that we’re all fine.” Since he was still suspiciously squinting his eyes at me, I had to throw him a little bone so he would leave us alone. “We actually saw some guy who was riding like a maniac in a tunnel, but he passed us by and we have no idea where he went.”

He squinted his eyes at me for the last time and left; without any proof, he was persuaded to get into his car and let us go.

“You have a nice night officer… asshole!”

But I guess he still reported us to his comrades at the Staten Island tollbooth plaza, since they looked at our bikes a little harder and longer than they should have. Still, they couldn't do anything. Willy, the nut, left his bike at Grossberger's friend's garage, where they repainted it and fixed it so it looked like new, and the next Monday Willy was more than ready to do it all over again. Such an insignificant thing as making fireworks out of your bike and some petrified guy's car never stopped us, Brooklyn and Staten Island guys, from repeating it all over again, trying to break our own records.

Very soon the New York City bike adventures weren't fun enough for the extreme-loving Renzo and Grossberger, and they started venturing farther and farther from home, looking for new biker towns to make their new playgrounds. They would leave early in the morning to find themselves in a completely strange new town in just a couple of hours, and the first thing on their list was of course to find a good bar.

It was one of those days, and Renzo and Grossberger were the first customers at some bar on the way heading upstate, which just happened to open its doors for the day earlier than everybody else in town (a decision the manager regretted later that day). After several hours of drinking, Grossberger started getting loud (a habit that none of his friends could actually control and none of the people around him would normally say shit about if they didn't want to get their asses kicked of course), but this time the bar manager decided to be a hero and stepped forward to calm down the rowdy customer. Renzo thought it was brave, but a very stupid idea, as well.

"Don't you think you guys had enough to drink today?" the manager said. "It's not too safe to ride a bike in the condition that you're currently in, so maybe it's time for you guys to go home and take a little break?"

Grossberger slowly turned around on his barstool to look at the guy who obviously didn't care too much for his life if he actually thought it was a good idea to ask the 300 plus-pound monster and his killer-looking friend out of his bar.

"And who the fuck do you think you are to tell me if I had enough to drink or not? Are you the surgeon general, maybe?"

"No, sir, I'm just the manager of this place, and I think—"

Grossberger clearly wasn't interested in what the guy thought, so he interrupted him in the most mouth-shutting manner that only he was capable of. "So you're not the surgeon general, are you?"

"No, sir, I'm not. But—"

The manager's "but" didn't interest the giant either, and he proceeded with his conclusion.

"If you're not the surgeon general, neither me, nor my friend here give a flying fuck about your advice on our drinking. And even if the country's most important surgeon general was here, I would tell him the same thing I'm going to tell you right now: get the fuck out of the bar before I make you eligible for disability payments. Got it?"

The bar manager got it surprisingly fast and left the bar right away, as advised by the very menacing-looking Grossberger.

"Buddy, what the hell was that? Did you just kick the manager out of his own bar?!" Renzo said, and couldn't help but start laughing.

"He was being an asshole, so I suggested he should go."

Grossberger's second victim was the bar cook, who was stupid enough to bring him an over-fried burger and pretty lousy French fries. Getting poorly cooked food wasn't unheard of, of course, but when Grossberger called the cook over and asked him (nicely, it should be noted here) to bring him a new portion and this time make it taste like actual food and not a piece of horse meat, the guy decided to get cocky and advised Grossberger "not to eat it if he didn't like it." Grossberger advised the guy to leave the fucking bar as well, before he would stuff his sorry ass with the infamous burger and make him the official Thanksgiving turkey of the town.

"Buddy, what the fuck?!" Renzo said. "You made the chef leave too?! Don't kick the bartender out… we still need him at least!"

"I won't, as long as he behaves." Grossberger smirked, and the two friends kept drinking for several more hours before they finally decided to hit the road back home.

"Don't you guys want to stay in a local hotel or something?" the bartender, the only remaining member of the personnel, asked them after they paid their tab and left him a very generous tip. "It's pouring outside, I don't think you guys can ride in this weather."

"We'll be fine, buddy." Renzo was already as drunk as his friend, and when he was in such a condition, he wouldn't even really care if tornados were destroying the town; he would still get on his bike and ride as if it was the nicest day out.

This time, however, the rain was really coming down in buckets and after hardly making their way back to Staten Island, soaking wet from head to toe, with all the passing cars beeping at them, the two nuts finally made it to their common friend's bar not too far from their houses.

"Are you two fuckin' guys insane ridin' in this weather?! It's a fuckin' hurricane out there!" Tim, the owner of the bar, always knew how to nicely greet his customers, especially these two.

"We're fine, just give us a drink!" Renzo said. After riding for almost two hours in the storm, the two friends had gotten almost completely sober and were now freezing their asses off.

"Where the hell are you two coming from?" Tim asked, fixing his signature drinks that were known for tasting great but fucking people up without warning—that's how much alcohol he used.

"Upstate." Both guys answered in unison.

"Upstate?! You two psychos rode all the way from fuckin' upstate?"

"Yep," Renzo said. "We were feeling no pain when we left that bar, and when we realized that it wasn't such a good idea, it was a little too late. So here we are." He gave Tim his little innocent boy's smile, and the owner just shook his head.

"I've seen crazy people in my life, but you two just officially broke the record."

"Cheers to that, I guess?" Renzo couldn't stop joking and goofing around even after almost killing himself riding in the heaviest rain all the way from the mountains.

After almost ten hours of drinking, they finally got home, but both got so sick the following day that they couldn't go to work for almost a week after their upstate drinking adventure. But when their biker buddies later asked them if it had been worth it, both answered without blinking an eye, "Yeah... Totally!"

Messing with the police after getting drunk was another fun activity on the wiseguys/bikers club's list, and the main instigator was Grossberger of course. He had his favorite trick that he would always gladly play on the cops that amused him and his buddies. He would get on his bike last, after all his friends were on their bikes, and while passing the annoying police, he would stop for a moment and make his back wheel spin so fast that it would smoke the whole block out, leaving the cops coughing and cursing at the giant. But by the time the smoke would clear, they would all be long gone and laughing.

This one time, when the crew was hanging out in some small biker town upstate New York, the sheriff himself decided to pay a visit to the City gang and walked inside the bar as if he was in the frigging Wild West.

"Are you guys here to make any trouble?" the sheriff said.

Since everybody was having a good time and wasn't really drunk yet, no one offered the sheriff their usual advice "to get the fuck out of their bar," and so they replied, "No, sir, we're just here to have a good time, don't worry about us. We won't cause any trouble."

"All right then. But keep in mind I'll be watching you boys."

With those words the sheriff walked out of the bar and proceeded right back to his car parked across the street from the bar, where he sat the entire time while Renzo and his crew continued carrying on inside. Grossberger, however, didn't appreciate such close surveillance, and right after everybody finally got on their bikes and was ready to leave, he drove up to the sheriff's car and knocked on the window. Too bad for the sheriff that he rolled it open, because at the same moment Grossberger pulled his favorite maneuver and filled the inside of the sheriff's car entirely with smoke. Renzo just laughed, shook his head at his nutty friend and took off with the rest of the guys. *This guy will never change!* he thought to himself and smiled.

The truth was that not only did Grossberger not mind the danger, but he actually was getting some sick kick out of each potentially dangerous situation he put himself in. That's why he bonded so much with Renzo, who was from the same extreme-loving breed, and together they made quite an insane item, the mere sight of which could make people pull off the road to let the two pass.

One time they headed all the way from Naples, Florida, where they had sent their bikes prior to the trip, to the Florida Keys. The idea was to get to the Keys by sunset and to witness what some people call one of the most beautiful sunsets on the East Coast. But prior to taking off on their trip, the two friends stopped by a local bar to have a quick dinner and a couple of drinks. A couple of drinks in those two guys' case meant at least eight, so after a while they started carrying on, entertaining the people around them, making some new friends and talking to the bartender.

When the bartender found out where the two crazy Brooklyn guys were heading at night, he was petrified.

"You're going all the way to the Keys at night?! Are you, guys, nuts?! The only road that leads there crosses Alligator Alley for a good hour. Are you at least aware of the fact that all those ugly reptiles have a tendency to come out at night and cross the road?"

Grossberger's usual answer followed. "We'll be fine, don't worry about us."

"We've seen things way worse than reptiles in our neighborhood," Renzo said, "believe me!" He laughed, finished his drink and, after paying his tab, left the bar, followed by his massive buddy.

The daily Florida heat had dropped, and the two friends enjoyed riding in the nice cool breeze for about an hour before they reached Alligator Alley. At first they just laughed about "the local pussies" who were afraid of a couple of tiny crocodiles, but the deeper they got into the alligators' territory, the bigger the reptiles were, crossing the road through holes and gaps in the fences that would supposedly keep them out.

Soon they had to maneuver around them like they were at an obstacle course; after another hour of riding, when the size of the reptiles could easily compete with the size of Grossberger, they started praying that their bikes would not break down in the middle of this mini-Jurassic Park. They finally realized that the whole riding through Alligator Alley in the pitch-black of night idea wasn't such a good one, after all, when several especially hungry alligators snapped their teeth at the bikers, obviously trying to catch their legs. In order to prevent that from happening, the two friends increased their speed and hoped that Alligator Alley would soon be left behind with all its creatures.

They say God always looks after the craziest daredevils, and this time Renzo and Grossberger got lucky enough to get out of it alive. But both came to the silent agreement to never repeat the night trip again. They grew up knowing how to deal with the local knuckleheads from New York, not the hungry beasts from Miami. It would be a great story they could tell over and over again, but after seeing the sunset, which turned out to be just as beautiful as everybody had described, they were more than happy to return home to their neighborhood. After all, they were Brooklyn boys, and very proud of it.

Chapter 8

"Renzo's Independence"

"If by some chance an honest man like yourself made enemies they would become my enemies."

(M. Brando as Don Corleone)

Renzo and his father, Frank, always had quite an interesting relationship. Maybe their sort of relationship wasn't actually so unusual for Sicilian kids, who were used to being disciplined by getting beatings from their fathers to the point where it didn't even faze them anymore. But Renzo, who had grown up in America, had no idea why he was the one who always had to "get it," even if technically he didn't do anything wrong. For example, when his crazy, Woodstock-charged, Beatles-obsessed and sometimes drugged out sister would get home after yet another party and pass out on her bed, Renzo knew his ass was going to be kicked, and all because of the Sicilian law prohibiting Frank from touching a woman.

As soon as she would enter the door looking all fucked-up, I expected the upcoming storm. My dad was so tough and had such a strong, loud voice when he started yelling that no guy would have had enough balls to cross him. But my sister was smart, she knew he would never touch a hair on her head. So she did pretty much whatever she wanted and would always get away with it. My father hated when she would come home high, he yelled so loud that I'm pretty sure the whole block could hear him. And what do you think that broad would do? Laughed in his face and told him to go fuck himself! What can you do? It wasn't her fault, she was a 60's kid and they were all crazy.

After that, as if nothing happened, she would go to her room and happily pass out on her bed, while my dad would literally trash her whole room; he'd break her record player, smash everything he saw, just go wild. And after that if he saw me, just sitting in the living room and not even doing a thing, he would give me the hardest smack and yelled, "What are you laughing at?!"

There was no point in trying to prove to him that I wasn't laughing—I almost wasn't even breathing. And that would anger him even more, and then I would really get my ass kicked! So I would just get smacked and be happy that it was pretty much over.

Frank had his own reasoning regarding "tough love" and child raising: "I don't want him to grow up a sissy who can't even stand up for himself! He shouldn't be afraid of anybody or anything, then I'll know I did a good job as his father!"

He probably knew what he was talking about, since his own father and him would quite often get into real fist fights and beat the shit out of each other on any occasion they disagreed over something. And while Frank's father would hold his son's head in a headlock and punch him, Frank would just laugh and say, "Is that all you got, old man?! Come on, you gotta do better than that!"

It looks like Frank really did a good job as Renzo's father, as Renzo grew up a real maniac, with no fear and no common sense whatsoever when it came to fighting. But their constant head-butting still occasionally happened and working at the family sign business only contributed to it. Frank was one of those bosses who only have two rules that his workers, including his son, should obey—rule number one: the boss is always right. Rule number two: if the boss is not right, see rule number one. When Renzo was younger, that rule worked pretty well, especially when Frank would send him to New York's toughest areas to measure and later install a job. It helped that Frank had another golden rule for his boy: "If you don't install that job today, don't even bother to come back!"

And it didn't matter if it was New Year's Eve, ten degrees outside and none of the parts were fitting for the installation. Renzo and his crew would take turns trying to warm their hands in their truck, and after almost eight hours of work they would finally get it done.

Renzo's crew took pride in their work, as the signs or billboards they installed were famous for being indestructible. One time when a gas leak led to an explosion of a building on Sullivan St. called Nucarone's Funeral Home, breaking every glass window in a radius of a hundred feet and leveling the entire building itself, Renzo's sign survived right next door at The Sullivan St. Theatre (which was the original home to the play "The Fantastiks" for many years). It just needed some dusting off, and it remained there for many years to come. Hearing about that, Frank just shrugged and said, "OK, son, you did a good job… but don't let it go to your head. Every job should be done like that!" Giving praise obviously wasn't Frank's strong suit.

As the years passed and Renzo became a grown man who was a father himself now, he got pretty tired of the role as Frank's gofer in the family business. He didn't mind the subordination and was fine with Frank being the boss, but Frank's treatment of him and his habit of giving orders definitely had to go. So the day finally came when it had to be settled once and for all.

I don't even remember how it all started, but he was being disrespectful to me in front of my own workers. It was just the last straw. I finally couldn't hold it in anymore and started yelling at him, "I named my son after you, and you are treating me like this?!"

We both got into each other's face probably for the first time in my life. I guess I just realized that I no longer had any fear of him… So I pointed to my jaw and said very quietly through my teeth, "Go ahead, hit me right here, come on!"

At that moment, he backed off. Again, for the first time in my life I think. After that I finally gained his respect, and I remember him saying how he had created a monster. It was funny to hear it from him. Still, I knew that we couldn't work together anymore; it was time for us to go our separate ways. And that's when my friendship and business partnership with Richard started.

When Renzo first met Richard (the same Richard who was later hanging off his boat), Richard was running a New York based sign and billboard company. It was the perfect opportunity for Renzo to start his own sign and billboard company separate from his father and together with Richard. The problem was that Richard already had a partner, or let's just say a wanna-be mob associate share-holder, named Jack, who wasn't a nice guy to begin with, but who completely pissed Renzo off when Renzo found out that Jack had been successfully pocketing Richard's hard earned money at every possible opportunity.

Jack's scheme was very simple: he would sell a sign to a customer at one price, present Richard a contract with a much lower version of that price and make the poor guy do the job with almost no profit whatsoever. Out at dinner with Renzo, Richard finally started questioning his "partner's" job summaries. Renzo, with more than twenty years of experience in the sign business, told him right away that the guy had been taking advantage of him all this time, no doubt about it. Now the main problem for Richard was how to nicely get rid of his so-called "partner." He wanted to avoid getting into any trouble; he was an honest, legitimate businessman, who unlike Renzo wasn't used to giving Brooklyn guys beatings right and left every chance he had.

Richard actually wasn't the first friend who Renzo helped break free from an unwanted "partnership"—the first was his childhood "brother from another mother" Giovanni "So-so." And the best part was that pretty soon all three Italians became almost inseparable.

It's always interesting how you make new friends: someone moves to your block, starts hanging out where you hang out and if he's cool with the rest of your crew, you become friends. That's how it normally worked in the old days in Bensonhurst. But since "normal" and "Renzo" never went hand-in-hand (and can actually be considered antonyms), the little Italian would always find quite extraordinary ways to make friends. And here's the story of his first encounter with So-So.

So-So wasn't the boy's real name of course, it was Giovanni, but as soon as you move to a predominantly Italian area, be prepared to get a nickname that will most likely stick with you for the rest of your life (or until you move away, and even then there will still be a pretty good chance that even somewhere in Minnesota you will meet a guy who's brother came from the neighborhood as well and who was married to a sister of the owner of the bakery on the corner of the house where the uncle of your brother-in-law still lives… and who knows you under the name of So-So—and this nickname will continue to gladly follow you wherever else you choose to go). You see, Italians are everywhere, and they somehow know each other; even if you eventually want to go back to your native Sicily to live with goats, you'll still be called So-So because someone will somehow find out that it was your nickname in Bensonhurst, Brooklyn.

The boys started calling him So-So after a popular at that time cartoon character; it was better than being called Footsie or Smiley, so the boy was OK with it. His big family, consisting of a mother, father and seven kids, had just moved to the block, and Renzo had immediately spotted one especially pretty sister. As all the boys always did when they had a crush on someone, he started following this girl everywhere and bothering her in every possible way, which included teasing, braid yanking, bag stealing, chasing and all the other adorable signs of a ten-year-old boy's affection.

So-So, who was two years younger than Renzo (and significantly smaller than him), decided to put an end to this unwanted attention to his older sister, and just like any typical Italian boy, he one day stepped up to protect his family member without taking into consideration the difference in size and age between him and his opponent. Renzo never expected that from the little So-So, who grabbed him by his clothes and bravely yelled, "Stop bothering my sister, or I'll kill you!"

"You'll what?! You, a little weasel, are going to beat *me* up?!"

Sammy, who was almost inseparable from Renzo to the point in which even his own mother called them the Siamese twins, didn't want to miss a chance to show the newbie who owned the block and jumped right into action. So-So finally realized that his chances against the two older and bigger boys were pretty slim, so he took off like a bandit. Renzo and Sammy were very impressed by their new neighbor's running skills, which actually saved So-So every time he would come within ten feet of Renzo or his buddies as even they, the best runners on the block, couldn't catch up with him.

Chasing So-So soon became the favorite pastime of the boys and turned into a daily routine, until So-So's mother, who spoke with a heavy Italian accent, finally confronted Renzo near her front porch.

"Renzo! Why are you chasing my Giovanni? What are you going to do with him?"

"Don't worry, Mrs. Lamberti, we wouldn't hurt your son, we're just playing with him! He got into my face one time, and we were just play-chasing him to teach him a lesson. We won't do it again, I promise!"

Surprisingly, Renzo kept his promise, and right after that little talk with So-So's mother, he took the boy under his wing and began looking after him. Not that he needed too much of a "looking-after," as So-So was probably the one good boy in a bad boys crew and tried to stay out of trouble as much as was possible hanging out with Renzo and his boys. But the older Renzo and the boys got, the bigger the trouble they seemed to attract.

When So-So's parents would leave for work and leave their kids home with their grandfather, Renzo would always find a way to sneak his new best buddy, Giovanni, out from the back yard as well as get him back home just before the boy's parents returned. Giovanni's grandfather knew all about the whole sneaking out business and was always yelling at his grandson in Italian, "Keep away from that crazy Renzo! The boy is trouble!!!"

But despite all the warnings, the boys soon became like brothers and would have done anything for each other.

Renzo has always thought that there's a special honor in protecting the weak and the innocent, in other words, people who can't protect themselves. So when his "brother from another mother," also known as the good boy from the bad guys' crew, Giovanni "So-So" Lamberti got in trouble with quite a powerful crew, Renzo couldn't have been happier to straighten things out for him.

Unlike his good buddy Renzo, Giovanni never looked for trouble and just wanted to work hard and take care of his family. But one day a big construction company owned by a "heavily connected" Italian went bankrupt, leaving Giovanni and many other workers with no jobs, no benefits, and no future. So-So, who had always been a smart businessman, put together all his savings, got a spreadsheet of all the needed expenses, started a new company and invited all the former workers to join him in his new business.

Thanks to Giovanni's professionalism and great salesman skills, the company started doing very well very soon, but the better So-So did, the more his success rubbed the former owner the wrong way. One day he finally showed up at So-So's door demanding half of the profits. When Giovanni politely questioned the "heavily connected" guy's rights to any part of his flourishing company, the latter got quite upset and promised to come back with his "business partners." Those "business partners" were gorilla-looking, six-foot-something goons with baseball bats who started camping out by So-So's office almost every day and terrified his workers so much that they were afraid to come to work.

As soon as Renzo heard about his good buddy's misfortunes, he grabbed a gun and jumped into his car without hesitation. After a quick chat with the "heavily connected" guy's "business associates" and a formal exchange of "who the fuck do you think you are" and "do you have any idea who I'm with," both parties realized that they were members of two different Brooklyn families, which didn't quite get along at that time. The only civil way to resolve the situation at that point was for their bosses to have a big sit-down and talk things through.

A couple of days later Renzo got a call from his godfather Rocco, who promised him that no one would touch Giovanni ever again. More than that, unlike most of the Italian "bosses," who often practiced taking a certain percentage of the business they helped to protect, Rocco didn't even ask for a dime, just as a gesture of goodwill to his Godson; a gesture that made Renzo love and look up to this great man even more. After all, it was Rocco who taught him that he should always protect the innocent, and Renzo never broke that golden rule.

Just like in the situation with Giovanni, Renzo was more than happy to flex his muscles and straighten things out with Jack without causing any trouble for his new buddy, and just a week later Richard was a free man, more than ready to jump into a new business partnership with his crazy friend Renzo. It was a business match made in heaven: the two partners were perfect salesmen with great charisma and personalities that won every customer over after only five minutes of talking to them. Their secret was that they weren't selling their product, they were selling their personality—and people loved it! They knew how to perfectly balance their deep knowledge of their business without sounding too nerdy about it; they joked around but didn't make an impression of being unprofessional.

One time they got a job before they even saw the customer (but it should be noted here that it was the customer who saw them first as they were sitting in the car next to his café and looked absolutely adorable fixing each other's ties). Renzo and Richard both preferred a casual style of clothing, but when it concerned their business appointments, they both agreed to stand out among the other casually dressed sales men by wearing suits and ties.

However, since both hated ties, they only put them on right before getting out of the car, and as both had trouble getting the tie knot right, they often helped each other with this annoying but necessary part of their wardrobe. During the whole process of putting on a tie, the partners would always play-fight, slapping each other's hands and screaming something like, "Are you trying to help me or strangle me?! Cause you're doing a great job suffocating me right now!!!"

This particular time they were really lucky because their customer was gay, and by watching the two in the car, the customer immediately jumped to the conclusion that they were without a doubt the cutest gay couple/salesmen he'd ever seen.

As soon as Renzo and Richard realized that the café owner thought that they were "together," they quickly exchanged a look with each other... and decided to totally roll with it. Who wouldn't when the job, which the guy was so excited to give them, coasted about five grand? After half an hour of pretending to be "the cutest salesmen couple" in the whole of New York City, the five thousand dollars richer Renzo and Richard left their customer absolutely happy and stopped for a drink at a bar nearby to celebrate and meet some cute girls. After all, they both were very good-looking Italian guys, but unfortunately for the rainbow community of New York, they were the furthest thing from a gay couple you could possibly find... not that there's anything wrong with that!

Getting a job so effortlessly by just pretending to be a little bit more than business partners gave the two sneaky Italians the idea to play this card for other people who would gladly buy into it. Both friends, who were always surrounded by girls, found this little game so amusing and easy that they could have easily gotten an Oscar for their performances. For example, when Richard needed to convince an unfriendly representative of a glass company to have a mirror fixed in his living room, Renzo gladly helped out.

“She’s not too friendly, Rich, what do you think?”

“No, not really.”

“I think she doesn’t like us because we’re gay.”

Imagine the poor blushing girl on the other side of the phone trying to convince the two partners that neither she, nor her company were homophobic.

“No, no, no! It’s not because… that’s not what I meant… I didn’t mean to offend you, I’m really sorry! We are more than open to work with… you know… I’m so sorry, what can I do for you, gentlemen?”

“Well, we need a mirror installed in our apartment in our dining room,” Renzo said.

“But we don’t want the ones with a beveled edge...” Richard’s perfect gay voice would put Perez Hilton to shame. “We want very good quality with a slight tint to the glass.”

“Absolutely, sir,” the girl said. “Let me assure you that our material is of the highest quality on the market, and you can have any beveled design or tinted color you desire.”

"That sounds fantastic, dear! Because this one time we were dealing with this other glass guy, and he was terrible! We ordered one thing, a pretty tinted one, and he got us something gray and yucky. Ugh, I couldn't even look at it!"

"Well, that's because he got upset with us, darling!" Renzo added; he was the "manly" partner and talked as if he were gay with a dead serious voice that was hilarious. "You shouldn't have been throwing your shoe at him! Then we would have gotten our mirrors the way we wanted them."

"Well, you shouldn't have been such a flirt with him," Richard responded, "then I wouldn't have had to throw a shoe at him! And for your information, Mr. Flirty Pants, I wasn't even aiming at him, I was aiming at you!"

"Oh, that makes me feel so much better, Mr. Jealous Pants!"

"Good to know, Mr. Flirty Pants!!!"

"Guys, guys, please don't fight!" the company representative interrupted, clearly trying to contain her laughter, but not too successfully, so she decided to pull her "gay couple" back on track. "So how big is the mirror you need and by when? And don't worry, I'll give you a very good discount."

The partners on the other end of the phone line exchanged winks and grins, and Richard said, "Oh, I'm looking for a really big one and would like to get it as soon as possible!"

Renzo's reply, "There he goes again… Mr. Flirty Pants is never satisfied!"

The easiest "customer segment" of the sign market for Renzo and Richard, however, was still the female one. As soon as a female business owner would shake the handsome Italians' hands, the job was basically in their pocket. Richard or Renzo would shamelessly flirt with the business woman, and after one of them climbed the ladder to measure the future sign or awning—letting the smiling lady admire "the view" from the sidewalk—she would sign up and hand over a check for whatever ridiculous price they named, without even asking for the full details of the job.

A problem they faced being happily single bachelors was that sometimes they would happen to run into business owners who also happened to be ex-girlfriends (mostly Richard's). Renzo was still technically married but also happily dating on the side, but unlike Richard, he preferred a relationship that would last a little bit longer than three to five dates and had been dating an aerobics instructor named Cady for several years.

The sign and billboard business was doing great, and the two decided to jump into the relatively new credit card operating business, going from store to store and offering the owners a contract with their company to set up a charge machine in their store. Everything was going just great for several months as Renzo and Richard gladly supplied Staten Island with their charging machines, until one day when they both were unlucky enough to walk into a lingerie store owned by Richard's ex-girlfriend Karen.

The look on her face said it all. Renzo knew right away that something was up as her face with its happy welcoming smile changed into something even more menacing than what Renzo was used to seeing on some angry, hardcore Brooklyn mobsters' faces. Richard, however, didn't lose his cool, didn't turn around and quickly walk away (which Renzo thought would probably have been the smartest way to handle the situation); instead he approached his almost fuming ex-girlfriend with a wide smile and the most confident look possible in a case like this.

"Katrine, it's been such a long time! How are you, darling? You look fantastic!"

"It's Karen." The tone the girl used would have been the same if she wanted to say "drop dead!"

"Of course it is! I'm just so taken aback by the way you look. I mean, you look just gorgeous, I almost lost my mind! How have you been?"

"What do you want, Richard? Why didn't you ever call me back??"

"Oh, straight to business. Aren't we past that?" It looked like nothing could break Richard's determination to sell his stuff, even facing someone who looked more like a fire-spitting dragon at the sight of her ex than the cute little girl she used to be before he had "exchanged" her for a better looking "model." "Great, I like that! My partner Renzo and I here are offering business owners credit card machines."

"Nice to meet you," Renzo said, trying to stay close to the door the whole time, secretly hoping Karen didn't have a gun hidden under the counter. Or a baseball bat. Or a knife. Or that she wouldn't just jump on both of them and kick their asses, because Renzo would gladly deal with armed Brooklyn guys, but not angry Staten Island ex-girlfriends, who, let's face it, can be way more dangerous and unpredictable.

"You got the nerve to come in here," she said, "and offer me some kind of a deal after what you did?!"

"Not just some kind of a deal, the best deal in New York City!"

"What kind of sick businessmen are you???"

"The very finest in New York," Richard confidently responded back. "We don't even have any competitors yet, because no one's prices can compare to the ones that we're offering! And since we're old friends, I can give you a great discount."

Here Richard even winked at the girl, completely ignoring her piercing eyes and ice cold tone. In his mind Renzo silently applauded his partner. Obviously, the seller's drive in Richard completely overpowered his basic survival instinct.

"Are you being serious right now?!" she said. "You dumped me without even explaining the reason, you just… disappeared on me, you stopped answering my calls, and now you got the balls to walk in here and push your stuff??"

"Karmen, dear, I didn't stop answering your calls…"

"It's Karen!!!"

"I lost my note book with all my phone numbers in it and my answering machine broke and I found out only two weeks later, can you imagine?" Richard was such a great liar that even Renzo was almost convinced by his sincere tone, even though he knew perfectly all the details of Richard's vow to "never pick up the phone if that girl calls again. She's annoying the crap out of me, and how needy is it to stalk a guy for two weeks now?"

"I would never do that to a girl," Richard continued telling his ex, "and especially to a girl who's so charming and so much fun to be around."

"Cut the crap. I've heard that story before. And I'm not buying it."

"Oh, it's absolutely fine if you don't "buy" my story, even though I'm being very truthful with you. But you should definitely buy our machine, because that's the smartest investment you'll make this year, I can promise you that!"

All this time Karen was nervously tapping a key chain with a large 3" solid metal ring on the end of it against the counter, obviously trying to take her frustration out on a non-living object. Richard, being a big flirt as always, playfully took it from her while still pointing out all the benefits she'd get from signing up with their company, and while the girl's hands were clasped in a praying position with both of her index fingers pointed upward, he decided to finish his brilliant presentation by swinging the ring around and looping it over her index fingers, smiling as charmingly as he possibly could. But the maneuver didn't go as smoothly as expected, and to Renzo's dread, instead of it looping around her index fingers, the heavy pendant cracked her front teeth as hard as possible. It sounded like someone holding a large glass goblet at a wedding and clanging it with a spoon to get everyone's attention!

"Uh-oh!" Richard covered his mouth, quickly coming to the realization that after this unfortunate incident his chances of selling anything to his former girlfriend were close to zero.

"Oh my God!!!" Karen screamed, holding her broken bleeding mouth, clearly looking more scared now than frustrated. "Am I bleeding? I think I'm bleeding!!!"

"Just a little bit." Renzo looked a little closer at the girl's wound without scaring her even more by telling her the truth: she was bleeding pretty badly. But even now his "inner jerk" just couldn't keep silent, and Renzo said, "It's kind of hard to see with all the blood, but I think you're missing a piece of a tooth…"

"Am I???" Karen looked like she was ready to pass out.

"Here, take this handkerchief." Renzo tried to save face for himself and his partner by being a gentleman even in a hopeless situation like this. "I think we'd better go."

"I'm sorry, Karen!" Richard made an apologetic smile while Renzo dragged him away before he could make the situation even worse. "I left my business card on your counter. Give us a call if you change your mind about the machine!"

"Let's go, you moron, before she calls the cops on you!!!"

After Renzo finally got his partner back to the car, Richard shook his head, saying, "I have a feeling she won't call us."

"You think?!"

"I suggest from now on that you walk into the store first."

"Your first good idea of the day, pal!"

The two friends bonded not only through their business partnership but also through a new healthy lifestyle that they both decided to follow. The drug era of the sixties and seventies was long gone, the eighties brought Jane Fonda and her aerobics and the nineties finally made people think of the quality of food they had been consuming without giving any thought to it. Renzo was now dating a pretty health-obsessed aerobics instructor and was kind of pushed by both her and Richard to follow this newest healthy lifestyle trend.

Richard was a runner, and for a long time he had been working on trying to make Renzo his running buddy. Renzo had played hard to get as always, but when on New Year's Eve both made a resolution to drop their weight from about 220lbs to their goal weight of 175lbs, Renzo all of a sudden was the first to put on his running sneakers. At first he couldn't run as long as Richard, but thanks to the latter constantly pushing him, in just a couple of months they were running five miles, then seven, then ten… till they probably beat all the records of the runners in Staten Island by easily covering a distance of fourteen miles twice a week. Richard would just laugh and say, "You know, you are the only man I know who takes everything he does to the extreme! You always have to be the first, the strongest, the best… and the craziest!!!"

The next step in their weight-loss program was a new diet, and very soon their pancakes and syrup in the morning were replaced by home-delivered egg whites and whole wheat toast from NutriSystem. In about a year the two friends were getting very close to their goal weight, but since Renzo was losing weight a little faster than Richard, he adopted the habit of calling his buddy "fat" at any chance he had; even though the difference between them was not more than ten pounds, Renzo couldn't stop his "inner jerk" from abusing his new best friend. Richard couldn't have cared less though and would gladly return the favor by calling his partner "fat" as well, just for old time's sake! So any phone conversation they had always included the most hilarious exchange of "pleasantries" like, "Fat, would you take the pork chop out of your mouth, I can't hear what you're saying!"

Or, "Could you call me back after you're done eating your pizza?"

And, "Remind me, since when are donuts included in your diet?"

But all jokes aside, Renzo was very grateful to his buddy for getting him on a healthy track. Drinking, however, was not on the list of things the two friends had decided to give up for the New Year; sometimes they wish they would have though.

They went to a training seminar in Colorado, which their credit card company held every year and their attendance was mandatory. Nobody said, however, that they weren't allowed to drink the night before the training day, so most of the sales associates used this chance to party as hard as they could. Since they were from all over the States, no one really cared how the people in Colorado would remember them. During happy hour at the local bars, all the uptight-during-the-day women in pencil skirts and business suits magically transformed into half-strippers, with their blouses tight right up underneath their bras and their skirts pulled up so short they left almost nothing to the imagination. The male associates, with their wedding rings in their pockets, were consuming alcohol like it was going out of style.

Renzo and Richard were right in the middle of that corporate celebration, which seemed more like a Mardi Gras after party than a serious salesmen get together. While drinking and carrying on like there was no tomorrow, the two partners at some point separated and only saw each other several hours later at their hotel suite. Renzo got there about an hour earlier than his buddy and happily passed out on his bed without even taking his clothes off. Soon though he woke up at the sound of his drunken out of his face partner struggling with the keys at the door. Renzo went to open it.

It was the funniest thing when I went to open the door for him! He was so drunk, he could barely stand, but he still didn't want to go to bed and was insisting that we should get another drink. But it only got as far as the vodka being poured into his glass; he got so sick just from the smell of it that he started making those gagging noises right in front of me. I started yelling at him, "Don't you fuckin dare throw up in this room, do you hear me??? I swear to God, you throw up here, I'm gonna strangle you!!! You want to throw up, go to the balcony and throw up over there!"

I gave him a garbage pail to take with him to the balcony (I wouldn't let Rich go to the bathroom after what had happened to my friend Peter at his mother's house when we had to hose it all down!). After about ten minutes he came back inside holding the pail in front of him and went to bed still holding it. The funniest thing was that when I tried to take it from him, he wouldn't let me have it! So we kept going back and forth.

"Rich, give me the fuckin basket! You're not sick anymore. You can't go to bed with it, it's a goddamn garbage pail!"

"No!"

"Give it to me!"

"NO!!!"

"Do you want to sleep with a dirty, nasty garbage pail next to your face?! Is that what you want?"

"Yes!"

"Good! Keep the damn thing. I hope you're happy!"

Now imagine that we both had to get up in just two hours and go to that stupid seminar and actually listen to all that crap for several hours! It was one of the worst hangovers of my life. When we walked into the auditorium, our eyes looked like they were bleeding, but most of the people actually didn't look much better than us! During the first hour, the president of the company spoke, but we couldn't have cared less and kept goofing around just because that's what we always did. We were the clowns of the classroom: every time someone asked a question or said something, we would make all kinds of remarks and comments and make everybody laugh.

We also had those books called *How To Be A Great Salesman*, and it was written by this guy named Ogg Mandingo. So Rich started playing around with his pen, and while the president was talking and we were going through pages of that book, my "good buddy" marked a passage in my book. I started whisper-yelling at him, saying, "Don't you dare mark my book!"

But he was being a smartass and wouldn't stop, so I started pushing his hand away, while at the same time putting marks in his book. We were play-fighting like that for a good two minutes, then he finally yanked my book away from me and started writing something on the first blank page. When he finally returned it to me, the signature he put there read, "Best regards, Ogg." I couldn't help it and started laughing. Rich started cracking up too, and we both just couldn't stop—you know when you get into one of those laughing fits? The president himself had to interrupt his speech and said, "OK, I guess we'll have to wait till the two kids in the back calm down."

Once Rich gets on a roll, he just doesn't stop, but he's so hilarious that you just can't help but laugh. The same thing happened after he checked those little hourly schedules they gave us that listed all the activities and saw his favorite word "lunch" in it scheduled at 12.00. Rich was quite disappointed when at 11.50 a female speaker walked in and introduced herself, so he said the following, which made the whole auditorium laugh, "Oh… I thought you were lunch!"

So overall the seminar turned out to be not as bad and boring as we had expected. Maybe it was because of us though… Probably because of us!

Chapter 9

"The Gentlemen's Club"

"I'm not the kind of person who calls the cops, I'm the kind of person that if you piss me off, you better hope you can call them before I get a hold of you."

(Unknown)

When you think about legitimate businesses that a Brooklyn goodfella normally owns, the first two that always come to mind are a restaurant and a gentlemen's club. This was why when Renzo came across an opportunity to join forces with his father's and now his friend Vito in running a gentlemen's club owned by his godfather Rocco, he knew he couldn't miss such a chance. First of all, he always liked to learn something new; second… well, there were very pretty girls there!

The club was located in a new place unknown to the public in the middle of the then almost uninhabited Meat Packing District, but it soon became one of the hottest and trendiest lounges in Manhattan. Thanks to brilliant management, smart promotion and the presence of "certain" individuals from Brooklyn, it became the favorite hangout of such celebrities as George Clooney, Sean Combs and the world's most famous athletes.

The girls working in the club all looked like top models, but the funniest thing was that it wasn't them who attracted the high-rollers to the lounge. The manager Vito and Renzo themselves were very approachable with the club patrons even though they didn't have to be, and people were fascinated by the idea that they could hang out with actual Brooklyn gangsters, as opposed to those guys who just played gangsters in front of people. Vito and Renzo would gladly buy their regular customers drinks (a simple gesture that would make them come back and spend even more money later on), and they took very good care of the discreteness and security of their celebrity patrons, for instance by always reserving a back entrance for their limos, which pulled up throughout the night.

The bar itself was quite the landmark: about twenty years ago, one of Mickey Rourke's first movies was filmed there, and the areas of the bar shown in the movie were left completely untouched when the new club owners had renovated the place. As a matter of fact, they used to constantly play the movie on every TV, and the customers got a kick out of drinking at the same exact bar where Mickey Rourke made his movie debut.

Unlike Vito, who was the top manager of the place, Renzo didn't have to spend every night at the club and would occasionally pop in just to entertain the customers and make new business connections. But celebrity or no celebrity, there was no way you could escape Renzo's pranks and playful abuse if you were lucky enough to hang out with him and Vito.

One of the funniest situations that all of their friends still laugh at included Renzo's cousin Larry and a dancer named Shyanne. The unsuspecting Larry was enjoying his birthday in the company of his friends, and after several hours of drinking and carrying on, he finally set his eyes on a strikingly beautiful dancer with a very exotic face. Shyanne had worked at the club since its opening, and both Vito and Renzo knew her little secret by then: Shyanne used to be a guy. However, thanks to generous "donations" from all of her customers and some fantastic work by the best New York plastic surgeons, Shyanne soon became one of the most attractive girls in the whole club. Her "private parts" though still awaited the ultimate change, but she knew how to mask it perfectly so that no one could tell there was something extra in her underwear.

After talking to Shyanne by the bar for a good half an hour, the already pretty tipsy Larry started winking at Renzo and Vito, tilting his head toward his gorgeous companion. When he came back over to Renzo and Vito, he was so excited, jabbing them with his elbow, telling them how much he thought the girl was into him. Renzo and Vito exchanged a look with each other and silently decided on what would be one of the best set ups in the club's history. So they started putting even more wood into the fire, pushing Larry to take Shyanne to the VIP room.

"Listen to me, buddy." Vito put on the most serious face he could in this situation, trying not to crack up. "I've been running this club for a very long time now, and believe me, that girl is never too friendly with anybody. I just can't believe how much she's into you!"

"Absolutely!" Renzo said, immediately convincing his cousin even more. "Look at her, she loves you! She just can't keep her hands off of you! You should definitely take her to the room before somebody else does!"

"It's your birthday, so we won't even charge you for the room. Just take care of the girl. And don't worry about the cameras, we'll disconnect the wires, so just have fun and enjoy yourself!"

Poor Larry was more than drunk enough to follow any of Renzo's stupid advice. So he took his pretty lady by the hand, and soon they disappeared behind the doors of the private room. Meanwhile, Renzo and Vito were laughing and telling all of Larry's friends how funny it was that after looking around for hours trying to find the best-looking girl, Larry had taken a guy to the room!

Vito kept his promise and did disconnect the camera wires that showed Larry's room, so it will always remain a mystery what happened between Larry and

Shyanne during those fifteen minutes that they spent together. But soon Larry ran out of there, holding his pants and screaming at his cousin and friends.

"What the fuck, man?! That girl has a dick!!! Why didn't you tell me nothing?!"

"We thought you knew that!" Renzo said. "We didn't say nothing because we all thought that you were into that shit, and we don't judge anybody. If a girl with a dick makes you happy, we won't discriminate!"

"I can't believe that you set me up like that!"

Even here Renzo couldn't stop himself and concluded this classic prank by saying, "Well, did you at least enjoy it?"

"Oh, fuck you, Renzo!"

At this point everybody was laughing so hard that tears were coming down their faces. And whenever Larry would come back to the club after what had happened, he would just stay by the bar and enjoy his drink; his private room days were over thanks to his cousin.

Renzo didn't limit himself to "abusing" only specific people; it could be family members, friends, customers or a stranger who he had just met—no one was immune to his witty persona. The funny part was actually that people would line up waiting for him to crack his next joke or do something crazy, and Renzo would never leave his audience disappointed. Even the toughest guys who he rode bikes with couldn't wait till Monday to see him. Monday was when all the Brooklyn and Staten Island Harley owners would meet by the last exit near the Verrazano Bridge and make their way to the club after having dinner in some friend's restaurant.

They chose Monday as their official hang out day since it was pretty quiet in the club customer-wise and there would be less people to be intimidated by both their look and bikes. Even the cops parked nearby, whose job was to make sure that all the drunk drivers leaving the club weren't too drunk to drive, knew that the bikers were with the club owners and weren't causing them any trouble. Some officers would sometimes even approach the crew and check out their bikes, all which were custom made and custom painted; each one was a masterpiece of bike design.

One of those times that a cop approached them ended pretty unexpectedly. Renzo and Grossburger had just left the bar and were getting on their bikes to go home, when a police car pulled up right next to them at a red light. The cop rolled down his window and gave the bikers a thumbs up.

"That's quite a nice bike you have there," the cop said, admiring Grossburger's gorgeous Harley.

Grossburger, who wasn't too fond of cops and never missed a chance to somehow challenge them, was this time in an especially adventurous mood, so he replied, "Twenty bucks to the next light!"

What happened next surprised both Renzo and Grossburger. The cops jumped the red light, floored the accelerator and raced down the road. The two friends quickly exchanged a look and in a split second were gone, racing to catch up with the cop car that was jumping all the red lights along the way (Renzo was silently thanking God that it was two in the morning and the road was almost empty).

The bikers and the cops were racing for a good two minutes at almost 100 mph, when finally Grossburger slowed down at the light near the entrance to the tunnel. The police car caught up with him and Renzo. They all looked like kids who had just gotten away with some petty crime, grinning and giggling; then Grossburger took it to yet another level when he reached his hand out to the cop car for the bet money. The driver laughed, smacked it and sped away back to the city, while the two friends entered the tunnel. Renzo was silently smiling and thinking that they weren't too different, cops and mobsters, and if he hadn't happened to have found himself on the other side of the tracks, he most likely would have been one of New York's Finest and been beating the shit out of people on a more legal basis.

Too bad that not every case of the bikers goofing around ended as well as the previous one. For instance, several years ago this one guy named Bryan from the Long Island crew got into a very bad bike accident, which ended in the surgery room, where the doctors successfully reattached his foot. Sadly, the leg was now a couple of inches shorter than the other one, but that didn't kill Bryan's passion for riding.

Unfortunately, due to his new condition, he had to quit professional bodybuilding, and within a couple of years he put on a lot of weight. Those little Monday getaways were his greatest source of entertainment at that point.

Sometimes, before stopping at the club, the bikers would have several drinks at Hogs and Heifers, and one evening their early party ended in the following way. The crew was making their last turn before parking on the sidewalk in front of the club, and Bryan, who was by then already pretty drunk, lost his balance, fell on his good leg and broke it. Since he was such a big guy—over 400 pounds—his buddies couldn't lift him up and carry him into the club, so they came up with a plan to get a wheelchair from inside and put Bryan in it before the ambulance arrived.

For some reason somebody brought out two wheelchairs. After putting Bryan in one, the crazy bikers decided to put Grossburger in the other, and they began organizing the most fucked-up races that only drunk Brooklyn boys could have come up with. Bryan, in one of the chairs with his broken leg, and Grossburger, laughing like a kid in the other, were holding on for their lives, their biker buddies racing them up and down the sidewalks, as one of the other guys was accepting bets on who was going to make it first to the club's entrance.

And again, the cops who were sitting in their patrol car across the street were just shaking their heads and laughing; they knew how nuts these guys were and just let them kid around (probably they were betting on their favorite guy themselves in that patrol car). The ambulance crew that drove up ten or fifteen minutes later was quite surprised to see their patient in such high spirits, and their driver even stuck his head out of the car and asked if they were filming a movie or something. After all, such a small inconvenience as a broken leg never stopped these mad men from having a great time.

Unfortunately, the club didn't live long thanks to the fine City of New York and its even finer laws about constantly changing zoning. With Chelsea Piers now built, it looked like all of a sudden the unpopular, and let's face it, quite unsanitary Meat Packing district with rats running all over it, was now flourishing and approaching its boom. And seeing the potential of the changing area, the city wasn't too happy that the gentlemen's club was right in the heart of it. Almost for a year the officials looked for a way to find some kind of violation that would give them the right to break the lease between the club and the building's landlord. Maybe it was because the owners didn't take the officials' warnings too seriously, or maybe it was just bad luck, but the city finally shut them down.

They say that when one door closes another one opens, and that's exactly how Renzo found himself buying a gentlemen's club in New Jersey. The previous owner, who was even a bigger coke head than all of his customers combined, wanted to sell the club immediately (probably because of the fact that he kept stepping on the same rake and marrying stripper after stripper, and each and every one of them took him for half of whatever he had). And when Renzo made him an offer he couldn't refuse (no, not a dead horse's head in his bed, but a suitcase with a lot of cash in it), the guy couldn't have been happier.

Right after all the papers were signed, the previous owner gladly retired, packed his stuff, married another stripper and moved to Florida, where he still lives when not in a rehab facility. Renzo, however, was left face-to-face with an almost dead business, drug dealers who seemed to camp out right in the parking lot every single night, strippers/prostitutes who for an extra twenty bucks were doing whatever the customers asked for, and a manager who had no idea how to run a club whatsoever.

Renzo always loved challenges. He decided that rather than trying to reanimate the business, which was more dead than alive, he'd better just start with a blank slate. So right after redecorating the place and making it look like a high-end Manhattan lounge, he fired the completely incompetent manager, installed cameras in every Champagne and VIP room, within just a couple of weeks got rid of all the dirty girls—who (if caught) would have brought him a lot of trouble with both the local police department and the township—and most importantly, he made the drug dealers understand that they were not welcome there anymore.

This last challenge wasn't so easy to complete though: both the drug dealers and the drug users didn't want to lose their great hangout spot and were quite hesitant to leave, to say the least. But they didn't take into consideration one simple fact: Renzo loved when somebody played the tough guy in front of him and couldn't wait to make the so-called "tough guys" cry like little girls and beg for mercy. Some of them were smart enough to draw some conclusions after Renzo's first warning; some needed a more physical explanation.

This was exactly what happened when Renzo noticed that something fishy was going on with a couple of black guys with nasty attitudes, who would come to the club almost every night accompanied by a couple of girls and would just hang out by the bar and do nothing the normal customers would do: they wouldn't get lap dances, wouldn't talk to the girls or order any drinks or food. Renzo got wind that they were probably drug dealers after watching their girls disappear into the ladies' room every half hour and the guys themselves visit the men's room way more often than they should have. *Either these assholes suffer from the worst bladder problems in the whole of New Jersey, or they're fuckin' selling drugs both to my dancers and customers*, Renzo thought.

After one more night of closely watching the suspicious individuals and after someone from the staff confirmed that they were actually selling drugs right on the premises, Renzo walked right up to them and said, "I know what you're doing, and I don't need this shit in my club. So you have two choices right now: you can either walk out of here and never come back… or you can get carried out. And make sure I never see you or any of your friends here again; there won't be any warning next time."

Just by looking at Renzo the drug dealers were more than convinced, got up, walked out of the door and never came back. But another time, some feisty Jersey douche bags, with very primitive minds, would only understand primitive physical power, and Renzo was more than happy to deliver. That night one particularly high on coke customer decided that the dancers weren't entertaining enough for the club and that the demonstration of his karate or martial-arts-wanna-be moves would spice up the atmosphere to the right degree. Unfortunately for this Jersey douche bag, he was throwing his "air punches" a little too close to Renzo and Vito's personal space (Vito happened to hang out by the same bar right next to the cranking idiot) and got them pretty annoyed.

Renzo, who was sincerely trying to learn how to control his anger around assholes and not kick every prick's ass, nicely asked the bouncer to escort the coke head out. The latter didn't appreciate this treatment and immediately got all his cockiness out, “Do you even know who I am, you motherfuckers?! I can kick any guy’s ass in this club! Do you want to take me outside?! Fine, you motherfuckers, let’s go outside, I’ll beat the shit out of you!”

The bouncer, who had either gotten too used to hearing all the same shit every night and thus simply ignored it or who didn’t want to mess with the Jersey douche bag because he knew the people he was with, just took him outside and left him there behind the closed glass doors. The asshole, however, didn’t want to give up without a fight and started calling out all the bouncers from the outside, bothering not only them but also all the normal customers, who were trying to have a good time.

“What, are you tough guys or not?! Are you afraid to fight me?! Come on outside, you little pussies, I’ll show you how to fight! You’re supposed to be so tough. Why aren’t you coming out, huh?”

If it had just been the verbal abuse targeted at the bouncers, the Jersey douche bag would have probably had a chance to keep his ass safe, but he made one fatal mistake that night: he started kicking the glass doors to Renzo’s club. At that point, Renzo completely lost his temper, and the Jersey douche bag’s last minutes were numbered. Renzo stormed outside in a split second and stopped face-to-face with the idiot, who had been disturbing his and his customers’ peace for the past ten minutes.

“I see you’re looking for an ass-kicking? Congratulations, you’ve come to the right place, asshole!!!” With these words Renzo, who acted as if he was throwing a left punch, caught the douche bag with his right fist on the eyebrow. After that, Renzo grabbed him by the collar and started throwing punches at the guy’s head without even meeting any resistance. After breaking the asshole’s nose, jaw and probably leaving him missing several teeth, Renzo threw him onto his white Mercedes parked right next to the entrance and let him catch his breath (or more accurately, spit out more blood and broken teeth). Surprisingly, the douche bag found the strength to get up (probably it was the coke still circulating through his system) and said, “Come on, motherfucker, I’ll kick your ass now… you want to fight some more??”

But no ass-kicking followed. After the guy lifted his fists into protective position, his eyes rolled up into his head, and then he passed out. Renzo just shrugged, ready to get back inside, when the Jersey douche bag’s friends decided to come outside and help their buddy. Seeing him on the floor completely senseless put them in an even feistier mood than they already were in, and it didn’t take long before Renzo started throwing punches right and left. Vito ran outside and started fighting the Jersey douche bags with Renzo. Very soon the Jersey crew realized that, even outnumbering the Brooklyn crew, which consisted of just two people, they were getting their ass kicked, and they quickly retreated to their still unconscious buddy's car.

"We don't want any more trouble!!" one of them said. "We just want to take him home, OK? We're leaving, we promise!"

Renzo and Vito respected the rule of the white flag thrown out by the Jersey guys, and they let them pick up their friend and leave. Needless to say, not one member of the Jersey crew ever came back to the club. The bouncers, however, were later called to the office, and after having a serious talk with Vito, they all got fired on the spot. The club's new manager Matt freaked out and started asking his bosses what they were supposed to do now that they had no bouncers, to which Renzo and Vito both answered at the same time, "We're the bouncers now. We clearly did a better job!!!"

Yet just another time that Renzo lost control of his anger, but he couldn't have been happier about it!

Not all of their problems came from inside the club though: both the Jersey cops and the township weren't too happy about the new club owners from Brooklyn. They were pretty much convinced that all Brooklyn Italians were automatically connected to the mob, and one evening they came to the club to prove themselves right. Too bad for Renzo he wasn't in that night, so Vito played host for the city officials; which almost resulted in Renzo's license being revoked.

Vito liked neither cops, nor any kind of city bureaucrat, both who he thought had nothing better to do than to stick their noses into his business, and therefore he always acted in a very condescending way around them. But even more than that, he enjoyed acting like the heavy-duty gangster that he was; it intimidated them and made them leave him alone. This time, however, the Jersey officials didn't get intimidated. On the contrary, they left the club annoyed and ready to shut it down as soon as they had enough proof in their hands.

The following day when Renzo got a call from his lawyer—who sounded very concerned and suggested that Renzo go and straighten things out with the city right away before they take his liquor license—he knew that he would need all of his bullshitting skills to make it out of this situation. Luckily, Renzo had the perfect combination of poker face/baby face and was also the most professional bullshitter in the whole New York and New Jersey area, so when he finally sat down across the table from the three city officials (who didn't look too happy), he was more than ready to play.

For more than three hours they bombarded me with all kinds of questions, trying to catch me lying, but I was just too good for them! They wanted to know what the hell was Vito, a convicted felon who was not supposed to be running that kind of business at all, doing in the office and showing them around. They were pretty clear that just this fact alone was more than enough for them to revoke my liquor license, so I had to put my most innocent face on and give them the "sad story."

"I'm just a sign man. I have no idea how to run this kind of a business, so I invited my longtime friend Vito to be a consultant so he would teach me all about it, since he has so much experience in this and I don't."

One of the officials jumped right on that one, "Do you know that your "longtime friend" is a convicted felon and a mob-associated person?"

I didn't even blink and went on, "Listen, I don't care about those things. He was a friend of my father's and now is my friend. I don't judge nobody and don't put my nose into nobody's business. He's always been a great club manager, and he agreed to help me out when I asked him to. If it's a crime that I asked for his help because I'm just a legitimate sign business owner and have no experience in running a gentlemen's club, then I guess I'm guilty."

My lawyer couldn't help but smile; I knew he was silently applauding me in his mind.

But those assholes didn't want to give up yet, "Well, in the papers that you submitted to the city you asked for the position of a manager for your friend. Now you're saying he's your consultant, what's that all about? Were you lying in your first statement?"

I laid the big, sad puppy eyes on even more and kept on bullshitting, "I'm just really inexperienced in this whole night club thing, you know? So I didn't really know what was the right wording for it. I mean, he's not technically a manager. We have a manager who has a schedule and works certain shifts, while Vito just comes and goes as he pleases. He just helps the manager out by giving him some advice and talks to the customers, that's all. I know that by law he can't be a manager, and I respect the law! He has no access to papers or anything, so I don't worry about it. So I thought I should change his status to a consultant, and that would be the right thing to do, just so I don't have any more problems in the future, right?"

They swallowed it all right up! My lawyer probably didn't even look as happy at his son's college graduation as he was when we left the building after three hours of that non-stop interrogation. One of the officials actually ran after me, shook my hand, apologized for the whole inconvenience they had caused me and reassured me that from now on they would leave me alone and wouldn't bother me with inspections or anything else. After my lawyer and I finally got into the car, he just shook his head and said, "Fucking Renzo! I swear to God, I've been practicing law for years, and I've never seen anything like that in my life! You should have been a lawyer!!!"

Sometimes I actually think I should have. Just by helping all my friends out I would have made a fortune!

Chapter 10

"The New Renzo"

"All I wanted was to be what I became to be."

(J. Gotti)

It's a funny thing how a person changes throughout his or her life: you meet new people, and these new people affect you all in their own way; they bring out new qualities in you, some just by being around you, some by putting you through situations that you never thought you'd find yourself in. Some make you stronger, some make you crazier, some make you smarter, some make you better. Renzo was a very lucky man, because he met them all. His two big influences were probably his father, Frank, and his godfather, Rocco, and the two of them certainly created a monster—one of the toughest guys in Brooklyn with a cute little boy's face, the perfect front man and a professional bullshitter. They taught him how to respect and be respected, what to forgive and what to never forget, how to be a fighter and a diplomat and how to win wars with a single smile.

His brothers "from another mother" Vito, Ben, Grossburger, Sammy and the rest of the crew brought out Renzo's crazy side and probably even enhanced it by always competing with each other, trying to win a title for "the stupidest thing I did this weekend:" racing cop cars, doing headstands on the famous "Cyclone" rollercoaster in Coney Island, having billiard ball fights in the Pool Room and street fights between gangs… Their motto was that if something was not life-threatening, potentially dangerous or wouldn't probably get them arrested, there was no fun to be had, and they lived by this motto their whole life. To this day, when they get together, they still toast to all the insane stuff they did and wonder how all of them (well, most of them) survived it.

His business partners Richard and Ralph made him love the sign business even more, sometimes by competing with each other, sometimes by playfully abusing each other and sometimes by teaching each other something new. Of course, Renzo would never admit that his partners knew a better way to do something and would always turn things around, telling everyone that it was actually his idea in the first place.

Both Richard and Ralph got used to that pretty quickly, and Richard would even playfully answer his phone by saying, "Renzo, let me begin by apologizing. I have no idea what I did wrong this time, but I guess I'm sorry. I was an asshole, it will never happen again."

Renzo and Richard's partnership came to an end when the latter got married to a gorgeous girl from Costa Rica and moved to Florida, where he raises a beautiful daughter and owns a successful billboard company now. But their friendship remains the same; they still talk on the phone every day for about an hour and Renzo still tells him to take the pork chop out of his mouth because he can't understand what he's saying. From time to time Richard comes to visit Renzo in New York, and they tell their friends all about the fun ways they used to win (and sometimes "con") their customers.

But they say the biggest influence on your life usually comes from your significant other, a person who changes you or makes you want to change for the better. Unfortunately that didn't work out too well with Renzo's first wife, and they got separated as their kids got bigger because they both realized that all they did was annoy each other; and that is clearly not a healthy way to continue a relationship. After several girlfriends and having nothing good come out of those relationships, Renzo finally met his soulmate, a little Jewish girl who was tough enough to deal with Renzo's crazy ways but patient enough to love him no matter what.

The little Jewish girl's name was Mila, and just like many female immigrants from Russia working in the gentlemen's club business, she was a hostess in Renzo's club. Renzo quickly forgot Vito's most important piece of advice to never get involved with a girl from the club because they are all the greatest con-artists you could ever possibly meet (based on fact in most cases), and he asked Mila out on a date. After a couple of months they were basically living together in a cute little apartment in Brooklyn and raising Mila's cute Chihuahua puppy, named Puppy.

After another four months of dating, Renzo became so possessive of his new girl that he made her stop working at the club where "all those guys are looking at you. I'll beat them all up" and made her a full-time housewife. Since then the two have become almost inseparable, and Mila is now driving around with Renzo whenever he has different appointments (even though her job description, according to Renzo, is just to sit in the car and make sure he doesn't get any tickets). Mila has actually become Renzo's entertainer and meditation guru on bad traffic days, making sure that he doesn't beat up some stupid driver.

Mila's opinion was that the whole fighting thing had to go, and she made that pretty clear from the very beginning of their relationship. Every time that Renzo would get his buttons pushed and turn into a fist-fighting Hulk, Mila would cross her arms over her chest and shake her head.

"Renzo Guarino... stop that right now and get back here! You are not fighting anybody today, so be nice, and get your ass back in the car before *I* kick it!"

Hearing those words from a tiny little thing like Mila was actually so adorably cute that Renzo would let all his steam out just by cursing out the unfortunate guy who had pissed him off, and then Renzo would happily proceed driving. But sometimes even Mila agreed that some idiot who shouldn't have been driving in the first place really deserved a smack, like that one time when they missed two green lights at a busy intersection because the car in front of them had a plastic orange cone in front of it and the driver didn't have enough brains to get out of the car and move it. She would let her intimidating-looking boyfriend out of the car—just like a personal pit-bull—to "explain" to the guy nicely that if he wouldn't get his "fuckin ass off the road right away, he would most definitely have it kicked," but she wouldn't let Renzo actually smack the guy.

The only real fight that was ever approved by Mila happened after the couple and Mila's girlfriend Emily were leaving Vito's new hangout, a very popular gentlemen's club in Manhattan. While Renzo (always a perfect gentleman) was picking up their coats from the coat check, some drunken asshole standing not too far away looked the two girls up and down and slurred, "Nice legs! Are you, girls, pros? We like prostitutes…"

Mila flipped him the finger and was happy that Renzo didn't hear the remark, as he would have beat the hell out of the guy right there on the spot, and then they would never have been allowed back into the club again. But fate is a weird thing, and the funniest things happen when you least expect them to: when all of them got into Renzo's car and started driving home, she told Renzo about what the guy had said and of course immediately got a disappointing look from her boyfriend because he had missed a chance to kick somebody's ass for a great reason. While they were stopped at an intersection not too far from the club, Mila spotted the impossible: the drunken asshole and his two buddies crossing the street right in front of their car! Before she even realized what she was doing, she yelled, "That's the guy!"

She covered her mouth right away, but that didn't help. Renzo was already parking the car on the corner in front of the guys, and in a split second he jumped on all three of them, throwing punches right and left. Emily, who was pretty shaken up by the whole situation, suggested calling the cops, but Mila just smiled at her and said, "Too late, he'll be done with them in a minute. And besides, that asshole deserves a beating!"

Mila was right. After easily handling all three of them, Renzo returned to the car and drove off before his victims could call the cops.

"I caught one right in the eye and clipped another's lip!" Renzo couldn't have looked happier. "They didn't even have time to realize what happened! Their friend actually wanted to shake my hand afterwards; I think he was just glad that it wasn't a mob hit and that I left them alive!"

The couple started laughing, and Emily just shook her head and said, "You two are insane!!!"

Now that Renzo's constant search for a fight was over and Mila could proudly say that her boyfriend was a lover, not a fighter, she had another bad habit to help him kick: she declared a cold war on Renzo's smoking. Being a very skilled psychologist, Mila knew that ultimatums wouldn't work with the stubborn Italian, so she developed a plan on how to make Renzo want to stop on his own. So after only six months of persuasion, mixed with medical facts and occasional alternative methods and psychological tricks, on New Year's Eve, Renzo smoked his last cigarette, and Mila celebrated yet another small victory. The funniest thing is that now Renzo is one of the biggest health nuts around. He keeps telling all his friends how smoking kills and how they all should stop before they die from lung cancer. Mila normally just sits by his side and quietly smiles. She absolutely agrees that Renzo always comes up with all the good ideas on his own (even if someone little and Jewish is inserting those ideas into his mind day-by-day, in little portions, so no one will notice).

After crossing fighting and smoking off of the list of dangerous things that could potentially be lethal, Mila suggested that Renzo cut out drinking hard liquor (which included his favorite, scotch and tequila) on the following New Year. Renzo suggested that she should just cut off his balls right then and put them on the shelf. However, after scratching the whole right side of his car while driving drunk and falling off the stairs in his house in Staten Island—cutting his leg on the metal railing so bad that the bone was showing—Renzo found that his girl's idea actually made a lot of sense and switched to drinking white wine even before the New Year.

Just when Renzo thought the "fun" part of his life (which included parties, friends and the whole "getting drunk and stupid" thing) was over, Mila showed him that he couldn't have been more wrong, and the self-proclaimed "Bonnie and Clyde of New York" quickly started creating their own crazy moments, which even their friends found hard to believe.

Since white wine was allowed and nobody said anything about the quantity of it (Mila was pretty sure that grapes are good for you, and Renzo would tend to agree), both would reach the limit when there were no more limits, except having as much fun as they could. So when they left their favorite Bensonhurst restaurant "Accaro's" owned by their great friend Don, the first thing they did was put the radio on full blast and start goofing around like two kids. Renzo had just learned that Mila couldn't stand her feet being tickled (and when Renzo found somebody's weakness, he wouldn't leave it alone), so he immediately grabbed his girl's foot, dragged it to his mouth and started playfully biting it.

Trying to get away from her crazy boyfriend, Mila climbed into the back seat of the car, yanking her foot away. But Renzo's grip was too strong, and he kept biting her toes while driving with one hand. Finally they stopped at a red light, and after turning her head to the right, Mila saw that they were sitting right next to a cop car. With that "what the hell are those people doing?" look on their faces, the two officers were watching her crazy boyfriend wrestle with her foot and continue to bite it.

Mila tried to yank her foot away again, saying, "Baby! Baby, stop biting my foot! The cops are right next to us, they're looking! Baby! Seriously, stop!"

Renzo couldn't have cared less or was just too drunk to think clearly; he wouldn't have let go of his girl's foot no matter what the circumstances had been. The cops, who had seen the couple so many times and probably knew them, just shook their heads, rolled their eyes and drove off as the light turned green.

It should be noted here that the restaurant "Accaro's" was their favorite hangout for a good reason: first of all, it was probably the most popular Brooklyn restaurant among wiseguy hangouts and circles (the fact that it was not known to the public as this kind of a place made it even more attractive); second, the food was always fantastic, and finally the company of "Accaro's" hospitable owner Don made the place simply irresistible. But sometimes when Renzo and Mila would come for a nice dinner, they got a different kind of evening than they had been expecting. One time they were sharing a table outside the restaurant with Don and his friend Jim, enjoying their delicious pasta and refreshing wine, when suddenly their pleasant conversation was very rudely interrupted… by a gunshot! It sounded very loud and clear, and judging by the sound the bullet hit somewhere near the roof.

While Jim jumped almost five feet off his seat and looked pretty petrified, Renzo and Mila just exchanged a look with Don. Then Mila took another sip from her glass and said, "Was that a gunshot we just heard? I'm pretty sure it was a gunshot…"

"Yep." Renzo was looking in the direction from where the shot had come from. "I think it came from that building. The pasta is really out of this world tonight, Don!"

"Thank you, it's my new recipe." Don smiled and after a moment added, "I'm getting mosquito bites out here, do you guys want to take it inside?"

"Yeah, let's take it inside."

It was just another Brooklyn law: even if you're getting shot at, you don't sweat it and you don't run for cover… But don't stay within shooting range for too long either!

Sometimes the couple's friends were "lucky" to be in the car when the two would start goofing around. One time Mila's girlfriend Mikky experienced what it was like to be in between the play-fighting of those two nuts. The three of them had just left Matt's boat party, and after more than eight hours of drinking they were clearly ossified. Nobody remembers who spilled the water on who first after getting in the car, but after Renzo and Mila ran out of water, having soaked each other quite well, everything within reach was immediately used to throw at each other. This included parts of clothing, change from the cup holder, gum, sunglasses, empty coffee cups, gloves from the glove compartment and even Renzo's socks, one of which landed right on Mikky's lap.

The next day, when Renzo opened the door of his car, he thought at first he had been robbed: the inside of the car looked like a bomb had exploded in there, and one of the socks was lying "dead" on the floor of the passenger's side. Renzo finally remembered what had happened last night and started laughing aloud. It looked as if the "fun" part of his life had only just begun and that his little Jewish girlfriend could easily outdo all of his crazy buddies.

Renzo and Mila would dress up and go to his club; then they would get drunk, get in the car and take a ride to a McDonald's drive-through and mess with the staff, who already knew them and would start giggling as soon as they saw their car.

"I'm gonna have a Big Mac meal," Renzo would say, "a small diet Coke, a muffin…"

"Anything else, sir?"

"Yes. Give me a McDick!"

"A what??"

"McDick."

They could hear the girl laughing on the other side of the speaker, but the funniest thing was that when they drove up to the pick-up window, another staff member would play along as well.

"Here's your order, sir. Enjoy!"

"Thank you! Do you have my McDick?"

"Yes, it's in the bag."

"OK, thanks!"

Just like the cops, the McDonald's staff would just shake their heads at the couple and laugh; people like that would totally make their night.

Even an ordinary thing such as a walk home after a party would turn into an adventure for Renzo and Mila. Who else but Renzo would kick all the orange cones along the way, because "if you see the cone, you have to kill it!" Or who else but Mila would have to prevent her boyfriend from climbing into somebody's garden because he would start saying that "they have daisies in there! I have to kill the daisies! I hate daisies! I was born hating daisies!!!" The daisy thing is not so crazy if you're in any way familiar with Brooklyn-Italian slang: when someone is talking about putting someone six feet underground, they normally say, "If that asshole doesn't get his fuckin' act straight, he'll be pushing up daisies in the blink of an eye!"

One night was especially adventurous for the couple when Renzo dropped Mila off in front of their place. She went inside their apartment, while he parked the car. On his way in, Renzo was so drunk that he couldn't handle even the lock on the front door, and he broke the key and found himself locked out of the building, with his cell phone forgotten in the car and the car parked in a forgotten spot. After contemplating for a moment on how to get inside, Renzo chose the backyard fence over the fire escape ladder and staggered toward the side of the building. It was around three in the morning, and the local possum was making his way to the dumpster; and here's where their ways met. The possum looked at the drunk Renzo; Renzo looked at the possum, wagged a finger at him and said, "Possum! I swear to God, you fuck with me, I'll make soup out of you!"

The way Renzo remembers it, the possum put his paws in the air and said, "Renzo, I don't want any trouble!" and then went about his business. Renzo climbed the fence and finally got into the building. The next day, when the super with a very grumpy face was changing the lock on the front door, Renzo made his famous puppy dog eyes and innocently asked what had happened.

The possum met Renzo a couple of months later; they shook hands and remain friends to this day.

Looking back, Renzo says that his life has certainly changed a lot since he met Mila: he finally met his match, someone who could handle him at his worst and therefore deserved him at his best. She calmed him down a lot, and one Christmas even took him to St. Patrick's, where he made his peace with God after years of being an uncontrollable beast. Renzo is still a force to be reckoned with, but now, instead of being ready to fight at every opportunity, he chooses to be a quiet power, just like his godfather, who once told him that he sees himself in his godson. Some great Brooklyn men reach that status when they have made a name for themselves and proved to everybody who they are, then they can finally enjoy their hard earned respect and the reputation that precedes them.

One thing didn't change about Renzo though: he knows where he's from, who he grew up with and who he should be loyal to. Such ties never break in a tight-knit Italian community, which is called a "family" for a reason. Years can pass, some

Brooklyn boys will get married and move away, some will have to do their time, some will be gone and missed forever… but no matter what happens, they always have each other's backs; and if a friend calls you at two in the morning asking for help, you'll get up and go with no questions asked. Because you know that when you're in trouble, your "family" will always be there for you.

They are the best of the best, the craziest of the craziest, fearless goodfellas, who despise the rules except the ones that the "family" lives by. They are the most loyal friends that you can ask for, they love with the same passion they fight with and many of them have went down in history, some glorified, some condemned by society; but people will keep making movies about the guys from Brooklyn and people will always have a fascination with them… This is a private club, and you can finally take a look at what's going on inside of it. This is Renzo's story about The Brooklyn Boys' Club.

The End

21647209R00122

Made in the USA
Middletown, DE
07 July 2015